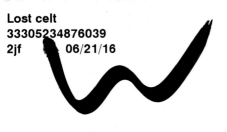

THE LOST CELT

A. E. Conran

GOSLING PRESS

©2016 Gosling Press, an imprint of Goosebottom Books LLC
Editor **Shirin Yim Bridges**
Copy editor **Jennifer Fry**
Typeset in Adobe Caslon Pro and Goblin
Manufactured in Malaysia
Library of Congress PCN: 2015942875
ISBN: 978-1-937463-54-0
First Edition 10 9 8 7 6 5 4 3 2 1

GOSLING PRESS

An imprint of Goosebottom Books LLC
543 Trinidad Lane, Foster City, CA 94404
www.goslingpress.com

Dedicated to the memory of
Tuesday Night Writer, Jon Wells,
the Peace Corps candidate
who was drafted into the Marines.

We miss you, Jon.

CHAPTER ONE

My Celts cluster together in the early morning mist. They lift their shields and flex their sword arms. Some of the men joke, but they're tense, I can tell. So am I.

On my right flank, Iceni cavalrymen jostle to be first in the charge. Behind us, at my command, a great horde of plaid-cloaked Brigantes spearmen stride into position.

When our battle horns finally blast their challenge, I pump my fist. Yes! My spies were right. Marcus Julius's Seventh Legion marches into the clearing from a misty dip in the forest floor. They appear, as if by magic, just where I was told they would attack. The rising sun is in our eyes and the element of surprise should be theirs, but we're waiting for them. We clash our sword hilts on our shields and hurl battle cries as if they were rocks. The amassed tribes of Celtic Britain are ready to rip the Romans apart!

"Surprise, Kyler!" I say, glancing up at his face in the corner of my screen.

"Oh man, no!" Kyler groans, trying to keep his voice down so his dad doesn't hear. He taps furiously at his keyboard, but it's too late. I unleash five units of swordsmen from the Trinovantes and Silures tribes. They charge in a blur of noise and fury.

Kyler leans forward, shaking his fist as he hisses into the screen, "I don't believe it. How did you get all those guys together, Mikey? How did you know about my attack?"

"Spies and gold, Kyler my friend. Pure and simple!"

His formation stays tight as my men launch themselves at the wall of red Roman shields—his legionnaires rank really highly on discipline—but then I order my spearmen to let loose, and it's a bloodbath. Kyler's Romans crumple under the rain of javelins, fighting to keep their lines as they advance over their own dead.

"Take that, Kyler!" I yell. Kyler's screwing up his eyes because he hates surprises, and I'm nearly jumping off my chair with excitement because he doesn't know the half of it yet.

I've just bought two whole units of Avernii. That's a tribe of Gauls, Celts from France; seriously scary guys with awesome longswords and, at ten solidi a unit, seriously expensive! And that's not even the best part. I've got a whole unit of Celtic berserkers, with a druid! They're my secret weapon. Anyone who plays *Romanii: Northern Borders* knows that the berserkers are awesome in battle, but totally unpredictable unless you have a

druid. Then they'll obey your every command and become invincible.

According to my military history book, "berserker" is a Viking word for guys who worked themselves up into a frenzy for battle. But the Celts did it too, just ask Julius Caesar. Tall, pale-skinned, and trained for warfare since childhood, the Celts were fearsome. They spiked up their hair with lime, covered their bodies in dyes or tattoos, ripped off their clothes in battle, and fought totally butt-naked, so mad on war and glory that no one could stop them. The Romans were terrified of the Celts and their crazy berserker fighting, but they admired them too. Too bad Roman discipline won out in the end. But not tonight!

Three months I've been saving up enough solidi to buy all the units for this battle. Three months Kyler's Romans have been kicking my butt, but tonight is going to be massive—awesome beyond awesomeness—and my Celts are going to win!

Kyler leans back in his chair. "OK Mikey, you asked for it!" He orders two units of Sarmatian cavalry to come storming down the valley to support his legionnaires.

"I'm not sweating, Kyler," I sing as I let my own cavalry fly. "I love poker night!"

Even Kyler has to laugh. Once a month Grandpa hosts poker night at our house. It's always on a night that

Mom works the late shift at the old people's home. All Grandpa's veteran buddies come over to drink, play cards, and tell war stories. They get so into it, Grandpa forgets to count my screen hours. It's the best night of the month.

My trumpets blare again. Kyler sends in two entire legions of auxiliaries, so I order my first band of Avernii up the valley, attacking his auxiliaries from the rear. Kyler screams in surprise, "What the...? Oh crud, Mikey. Where did they come from?" They're hacking his guys to pieces, and I'm laughing at Kyler's face on the screen when I hear Grandpa yelling my name from somewhere outside. It sounds bad. Real bad.

》 》 》

It's half past midnight, and Grandpa and I are still waiting to see a doctor. We sit in the emergency room of the hospital run by the Veterans' Administration, or "Vee-Ay" as Grandpa calls it, in a little cubicle the nurse made by pulling curtains around us. Grandpa's on a bed with his stick next to him. His pants have ridden up, showing a few inches of his metal prosthetic leg. On his other shin there's a gash and some dried blood. I'm on a grey chair with Dad's tablet on my knee. In the confusion after Grandpa's fall, I left my headphones at home, but at least Kyler and I put the game on pause. Now we've restarted, I'm still winning, and Kyler's still cursing me from his corner of the screen because this battle really isn't going according to plan—well, at least not to his.

"You sure you're OK, Grandpa?" I ask, looking up as the slimy plastic curtains billow apart. This happens every time the staff run by, which is a lot, by the way. It's busy at the VA.

"Should've picked a quieter night to fall down the steps," Grandpa says with a wink. "But, I'm fine. Those triage nurses did a great job, Mikey. You keep playing." He cradles his hurt wrist in an ice pack like it's a baby, but he doesn't seem too unhappy about it.

My second band of Avernii attack the remains of Kyler's cavalry, and it's a blood fest. Even men on horses are no match for my guys. Kyler cries out and then covers his mouth. His dad still thinks he's asleep.

Grandpa chuckles as Kyler groans from the screen. "Sounds like you gotta use your reserves, Kyler!" he calls. "Mikey's got you cornered."

"Don't give him any ideas," I say.

Grandpa laughs, and his whole face crinkles up like a wrung out dishcloth. "Heh, heh, heh."

Kyler takes Grandpa's advice and sends in all the legions he's been holding back at the edge of the forest. Wow! There are way more than I thought. Blocks of red shields march through his shattered troops. And that's when Kyler says, "Hey, Mikey, wouldn't you do anything to travel back in time so you could see this stuff for real?"

It's classic "Kyler Distraction Technique Number Five": hit me at my weakest point. "Not listening, Kyler," I say as his men flood into the center of the field.

"Like that guy we saw online who said the government's known about time travel for years. The one who said he went back to the Battle of Bull Run—"

"Still not listening."

"Through that electric tunnel invented by Tesla, and then he got stuck in the future for like two years, and all those physicists were saying it could really happen—famous guys not crackpots—"

"Not working, la, la, la," I sing as my spearmen hurl their javelins at Kyler's forces again. But the thought of being stuck in the past, or the future, really gets to me. What would that be like? Did that guy really travel to Bull Run?

When I glance back at the screen, I find my men in full retreat. This is so "Celtic armies." They can be winning one moment and totally routed the next.

"Hold the line, guys," I yell, but they've already scattered. Kyler's legions re-form and charge. I only have one chance. "This is the end, Kyler, my man. Say your prayers!"

I let loose my druid and unit of berserkers. They're all in amazing two-wheeled British chariots that can ride over any ground. Each one is driven by a charioteer. His job is to drive the berserker straight into the thick of the battle and then collect him again when needed.

"I don't believe it," Kyler gasps, clutching his head in his hands. "How did you buy them? You couldn't have saved enough…" His voice trails off in shock as the chariots zig-zag to block my fleeing troops. The druid waves an oak branch: it's a druid thing. The berserkers howl challenges and swing the heads of fallen Romans on lengths of rope: it's a Celt thing. Then the charioteers storm directly at Kyler's advancing Romans. The berserkers run along the chariot shafts while the horses are still galloping. They are totally naked. Their red hair is spiked up in all directions. They have large red mustaches, tattoos all over their bodies, and torcs—great twisted ropes of pure gold—around their necks and arms. They are magnificent.

They leap off their chariots, flying over the heads of the leading Romans, straight into the middle of the formation. No one can stop them. They're roaring and ripping the Romans apart, cutting great swathes through the legions, screaming war cries…when there's a whole lot more shouting, and it takes me a second to realize it's not coming from my screen.

I look up. Down the hallway, furniture—or something—is crashing to the floor. People are running from all over the place. Someone's screaming for medicine, and a woman is shouting for help.

"We can't get near him," she cries.

Two VA police officers sprint past the cubicle, shoes squeaking on the floor. They're running so fast the curtains billow right open and I see their uniforms.

Then, over the top of the noise, a man yells one word as loud as any battle cry. "Cuckooland!"

At least that's what it sounds like from where I'm sitting. He holds on to the last bit for a really long time, his voice deep and growly like a lion's. "Cuckoolaaaaand!"

Everything falls silent for a moment. Kyler asks, "Wow, what's up, Mikey?"

Then everyone's yelling again, and the guy keeps shouting, "Cuckooland!"

"Cuckooland?" Grandpa asks. "It sure is 'round here."

"What's that, Grandpa?"

Grandpa shakes his head and laughs. "Heh, heh, heh," he goes. "Gotta love the VA, Mikey. Gotta love it." It's the same laugh he always has on poker night when he's drunk a few beers. "Still, I should've just left the poop 'til morning, Mikey Boy. I knew it, but I just couldn't."

"Cuckoolaaand!" the man yells again, and I can't help it. I've got to see what's going on.

"I'm gonna go pee, Grandpa," I say.

"Sure, Mikey. Be quick, and don't talk to anyone. Knew I shoulda left it 'til morning."

Kyler yells for me to come back as I run through the curtains straight into his mom, Dr. Mariko Curtis. She works nights at the ER, just like my mom does at the old people's home.

"Whoa," she goes. "Is that you, Mikey?" She stumbles back and, for a second, she looks just like Black Orchid, the scariest lady ninja in *Samurai Sunset*. That's the Japanese version of *Romanii: Northern Borders*. Kyler's desperate to get it for his birthday, but his mom says one war game is enough. She's not falling for the "it's my heritage" argument.

Another doctor runs past. "I've got it, Mariko," he says, glancing between us as he hurries by.

"OK, I'll be right there." She looks a bit worried but still manages to smile as she says, "Dave texted that he'd brought you two in. I've been trying to get to you. Is your mom working tonight?"

"Yeah, and Dad's still in Nigeria—"

"Yes, I know—"

"And Grandpa fell down the steps outside our house."

"Aha," Mariko says. She glances down the hallway. Everything has gone quiet again. I really want to see who was making all the noise, but I should stay with Grandpa. So, as Mariko pushes through the curtains, I follow her in.

"Hey, Marty, how're you doing?" she asks. "I'm just checking in quickly." She gives Grandpa a good look and then nods at me. I guess she's telling me that he can wait a little longer and still be OK. "Did you hit your head when you fell?"

"No." Grandpa holds up his arm. "Saved myself with my wrist and cut my leg. Probably shouldn't be bothering you, but the boy wanted to come and I never argue with a redhead."

Grandpa loves my red hair and freckles. Mom says they came out of nowhere. Grandpa says they came out of England, and that's what you get for marrying a Brit. "And thank your Dave for driving us. The boy insisted we call Dave."

"He was right," Mariko says, because Mom would be furious if I walked Grandpa up to the emergency room at night, even if it is just up the street. It's our secret agreement. Mom always says, "If there's something wrong with Grandpa, call Mariko and Dave. If it's really serious, call the ambulance right away."

There's another crash down the hallway. I speak quickly. "Someone threw a plastic bag full of dog poop into our front yard. Grandpa saw it after he'd waved off his buddies."

"Dog owners," Grandpa grumbles. "Why can't they just take it home, like they're supposed to?"

"He went to get it, lost his balance, and fell down the front steps."

"Just the last step," Grandpa says.

"Poker night?" Mariko asks.

"Always lose my balance on poker night," Grandpa says. "Heh, heh, heh."

Mariko raises her eyebrows at me. "And where were you, Mikey?"

I hesitate, and maybe I glance at the tablet because Mariko suddenly leans over the chair, refreshes the screen, and says, "Kyler Curtis. Into bed. Now! It's past midnight on a school night, for goodness' sake."

She's shaking her head because she knows exactly what Mom thinks about war games, and Kyler is squeaking some lame apology, and Grandpa is saying, "The boys were just keeping me company, heh, heh, heh," when there's a whole lot more shouting.

"You can't do that, sir."

"Get down!"

"Don't pull those out!"

Mariko straightens up. "Sorry, Marty, I'll be right back." She runs off.

I shouldn't leave Grandpa, but the man yells again and I say, "I'll be right back, too."

I chase Mariko past the reception desk, down a hallway to a room on the left, and…whoa! How cool is this?

There's a guy, a really huge guy, in loose plaid pants and a hospital gown. He's on one of those big metal beds on wheels, squatting like a sumo wrestler. He shakes his fists in the air and flexes his biceps. He's got fierce, icy-blue eyes and wild ginger hair that sticks out in frizzy clumps. His lip is hidden by a prickly red mustache, and his chin is covered with red stubble. His eyebrows are thick and bushy, and he knits them together while he shouts. I can see the inside of his mouth, and it's a blood red "O." He stinks too; a cross between the laundry when Mom forgets to empty the machine and Grandpa's empty beer bottles.

I stick my head through the door to watch. No one pays any attention to me. The two VA police officers, the doctor, and two nurses are standing around the bed like a bunch of outfielders.

"Come on."

"You gotta calm down."

"Just get off the bed, now."

"We have to get him down," Mariko whispers to the others.

The police officers make a grab for the guy's arms, but he kicks out at them. One gets a boot in the side of his head. "Ooof," he groans as he falls to his knees.

"Cuckoolaaaand!" the man yells and rips at the tape on his arms.

The doctor's saying, "Not the IV! Not the IV!" But the man roars, and the IV line is out.

A machine starts beeping. Then he rips off the gown. And I don't mean taking his arms out of the sleeves one at a time. No way. I mean he just rips the front off with his bare hands and throws it across the room. A male nurse gets hit in the face. The man's arm swings back and hits the IV stand. The whole thing crashes to the floor, knocking over a jug of water on the bedside table. Water sprays all over the walls. An alarm goes off. The man shouts "Cuckoolaaaand" again.

This is the most exciting thing I've ever seen!

Now that he's pulled off the gown, I can see this guy is in really good shape. His chest is solid with muscles, and his skin is covered in tattoos. Thick bands of blue ink circle each of his forearms and—wow!—his chest is one big swirl of lines: long, thin animals turn in and out of themselves like knots. He's a walking graffiti wall and, here's the most amazing thing, around his neck he wears a twisted metal torc.

The minute I see it, my mind whirls. I mean, who wears a torc in California? This guy's a warrior, a Celt. In fact, he's the best type of Celt—a berserker just like my guys in *Romanii: Northern Borders*. They were the most feared of warriors. They were the best, and I'm watching a Celtic berserker, right here, right now.

Kyler will never believe me! I grab my phone to take a picture when the warrior lets out this massive cry. It's louder than anything so far. It's like an order in a language I don't understand.

I freeze, phone in hand.

He points right at me, his eyes pleading, and he yells, "Not this time!"

CHAPTER TWO

"What are you doing, Mikey?" Mariko throws herself in front of me and hustles me back to the door. "You shouldn't be seeing this! You shouldn't be here!" She keeps shielding me and pushing me toward the hallway. "You might get hurt."

The warrior glances around, his eyes wide, and I can tell he's really confused. I would be too, if I were him. I scan the room. There's no time-travel machine or anything that I can see, no portal, no wrinkle in time, so I don't know how all this is working, but this guy must be really freaked. There were no hospitals in his time, no syringes or IV lines, none of this stuff.

"It's OK. It's safe," I say, peering around Mariko's white coat. Mariko shushes me, but I wriggle to one side so I can see the warrior better, and I keep talking. "You're in a hospital. The VA. My grandpa's here, too. He says the VA may have its problems, but they've always treated him right." I must be saying the right things because the guy looked like he was somewhere else, but now he's back, focusing on me. "Great doctors, Grandpa says.

Isn't that right, Mariko?"

"Yes." She puts her hand on my shoulder, and I can feel her shaking. "You're safe."

The Celt relaxes his fists. Something changes because his eyes aren't fierce anymore. They're a warm, bright blue like two penny-sized chunks of sky stuck in a face as weathered as our redwood deck, and he looks like he wants to cry.

The nurses swoop over to him as he buries his face in his hands. "I don't want to get stuck here," he says.

And that's when I know for sure that I'm right.

Mariko hurries me out of the room and down the hallway back to the reception desk. "Mikey, I'm so sorry. You shouldn't have seen that." She runs her hands across her forehead and holds the top of her head for a moment. "Oh, what a mess. What am I going to tell—" but then she stops herself, takes a deep breath, looks straight into my eyes and says, "Oh my goodness, Mikey, are you all right? That was pretty scary back there."

It's true, I'm shaking. With shock, I guess, but with excitement, too. I can't believe this is happening. "Yeah," I say. "I'm great. Just great." And all the time I'm wondering why Mariko isn't as totally astonished as I am.

A door creaks. I crane my neck to see. The police officer who got kicked in the face comes out of the room rubbing his cheek.

"Everything OK? Need me to take a look, Miguel?" Mariko asks.

"I'm good. Just need some ice." He shakes his head as if to say, "just another night at the VA." "Good job quieting him down, kid! What grade are you in?"

"Fourth," Mariko answers. "With my son, Kyler."

"Cool." Miguel makes for the break room, still rubbing his jaw. I can't believe they're all so calm about this, so un-amazed.

"But will he be all right?" I ask.

"Who? Miguel?" Mariko pulls the elastic from her ponytail, smoothes her long black hair, and ties it back again.

"No! The warrior!" I say. "The Celt."

"What?" Mariko looks shocked. She puts her hand over her mouth and shakes her head. It takes her a while to recover. When she speaks again she's kind of breathless. "Wow, you're right! He did look like a Celt, didn't he?" she says. "You nailed it, Mikey." She hesitates, "But, you know…I think he'll be just fine."

She's so casual. "Fine?" I say. "Fine? How can he be fine? I mean, does he even know where he is, and what's happening?"

"Oh Mikey," Mariko says. "You're a sweet boy." She puts her hand on my shoulder. "We'll help him. We'll work it out. Don't you worry." She pauses as if she has to be careful about what she says next and lowers herself down so we're on the same level. Mom does this when she thinks she's going to say something important, so I lean in. "You see, we've been dealing with this for years now," Mariko whispers.

"You have? You've seen more guys like him?"

"Yes, and a few come back again and again. Especially on certain nights, when there's a natural disaster or something. That's when we see more activity."

"Activity? You do? But how come we don't all know about it? I mean this is huge!"

Mariko gives me a sad smile. "That's one way to put it, Mikey. It is huge, and you know, I wish more people did know about it. Sometimes I think they don't want to know. It's like this…this…big secret!"

I can hardly believe what she's telling me. Maybe the shock shows on my face because she suddenly drops her voice and says, "Oh Mikey, I can't tell you any more about this guy. It's against the rules. But we'll look after him. He'll be OK. Really, he will. I mean, once you've experienced certain things they never quite go away. But people do get better. We'll help him. Don't let this worry you, OK?"

Wow! What does she mean, worry me? This is the best night of my life!

I look into Mariko's face. She seems really concerned.

I'm not sure what I should say or do, so in the end I just nod and agree that I'll talk to her if I need to.

I must have said the right thing because she smiles and straightens up. "Good. Come on, let's go find Marty."

She acts as if our whole incredible time-traveling Celt conversation never happened. But I was there. I saw him. Awesome doesn't get any bigger than this.

I can't wait to tell Kyler tomorrow!

CHAPTER THREE

Grandpa and I hardly get any sleep. Most of the night we spend in the ER. The rest I spend at home looking at time-travel videos online. How can I sleep when I've just seen a real live Celt?

The more I watch, the more I play back that conversation with Mariko in my head. Was she trying to tell me that there's a conspiracy, just like the videos say? That time travel is happening all the time, but it's a big secret and somehow she's involved? It gives me goose bumps just thinking about it. Can a secret that big stay a secret? I pull my military history book from the shelf by my bed. Wars are full of secrets, even our battles in *Romanii: Northern Borders.*

The proof is there in black and white. During the Second World War, no one knew the Allies were making the atomic bomb, especially not the "general public," even though whole "secret" towns were built where the bombs were made. And no one knew they had broken the Enigma code years before the war ended. Not even the Allied armies knew that the intelligence people had broken the code. Throughout history there have been secrets—massive secrets. This must be another one. Kyler's gonna love this!

I must have fallen asleep because I wake up, what seems like five minutes later, with the book still open on my bed and my alarm blaring as loudly as a fire engine. I roll over groaning and hit the snooze. It's only on the fourth burst of ringing that the memory of the Celt blows me clean out of bed like an electric shock.

Grandpa's already downstairs packing my lunch. He slides a bowl of cereal across the table as I sit down. Cereal without milk, just how I like it.

"How are you, Grandpa?" I ask.

"Sore. Pretty sore. But we had an adventure, Mikey Boy, didn't we? Heh, heh, heh."

I nod and shovel cereal into my mouth as quickly as I can.

"You're running late this morning," Grandpa says. "I was gonna let you sleep in. I already texted Dave to say you wouldn't be walking with Kyler, but now that you're up...can you hustle?"

"Sure! Maybe I can catch up with him."

I finish my cereal in record time, and I'm just putting my lunch box in my backpack by the door when Mom comes in from her shift. She makes me even later by doing what Grandpa calls one of her "Spanish Inquisitions."

This means she goes ballistic and asks lots of questions that neither Grandpa nor I get the chance to answer before she's on to the next. You can bet Mariko's already texted the details, but Mom insists on hearing them again from us.

"Poker night, Dad? On Sunday night? When Mikey has school the next day?" Mom speaks really fast when she does the Spanish Inquisition.

"It was the only night all the guys could make this month—"

"And you go down unlit steps?"

"There was dog poop in the—"

"You could've broken your arm, or leg, or both."

"It's just a strain, and a few stitches—"

"Were you drinking?"

"I had two or—"

"You go down unlit steps when you've been drinking?" Mom slaps her forehead like she can't believe what she's hearing.

"There was a plastic bag of dog—"

"And you couldn't leave it 'til morning?"

"Yeah I shoulda—"

"And Mikey was still up? On a school night?"

"He was in his bed—"

"Who called the ambulance?"

"Dave drove us—"

"And you let Mikey stay in the emergency room?"

"Dr. Curtis was—"

"He couldn't have stayed with Dave?"

It goes on and on until she's just shaking her head saying, "I don't believe it, Dad. I just don't believe it. I come home from work, and I'm still at work. What can I say? What am I going to do with you?"

She slugs back black coffee even though she never drinks coffee after a shift. While her mouth is around the cup, I make a dash for the door. "Don't forget your phone, Mikey," she calls. Grandpa limps after me.

"Don't worry, Mikey. I'll set her straight," Grandpa says. "Mom's not mad at you, but I'm in the dog house for sure. Throw me a bone next time you see me, heh, heh, heh."

》 》 》

I make it to school with half a minute until the bell. Probably because I'm late, Kyler's playing with the "tetherball kids" in the yard. The tetherball kids are always out there right up to the bell.

"Kyler!" I yell from the far side of the blacktop. "You'll never guess what I saw last night!" I run to meet him, my tin lunch box clanking in my "mom-disapproved" camouflage backpack, but before I can reach him the bell rings.

"Come on, you'll be late," he yells as he joins the last kids racing headlong for class.

There's no time to talk as we stuff our backpacks into our cubbies and sit down at our table for roll call, but the minute Miss O'Brien gets behind her computer to email our class numbers to the office, Kyler says, "What happened? You left the game!"

"Oh man, did you put it on pause? Did I win? Did I miss my entire victory?" I can hardly believe myself. I have the most super-amazing news in the world, and this is the first thing that comes out of my mouth.

"No," Kyler says. "You didn't miss anything. I put it on pause." He shakes his head as if he knows he's the best friend ever and kind of wishes he wasn't right now.

I try to thank him, but Miss O'Brien starts her Monday morning routine, announcing who's paper collector, who's librarian, all that stuff. There's no way I can tell Kyler anything while she's talking. It's torture. I keep thinking she has to take a breath sometime, but no. It appears Miss O'Brien has given up breathing this week because the moment she's done with the "helpers," she says, "And now it's your favorite Monday morning moment: what does Monday morning mean?"

"Math!" the class shouts.

"Yep, it's quiz time!"

Everyone cheers and then, remembering they're supposed to be upset, they groan. Casey Rubens, sitting across from me, pretends to barf into her pencil case.

"Oh, come on! You love it!" Miss O'Brien shakes the candy jar on her desk. "And today's special question will be…" She takes two dice from her desk drawer and rolls them while everyone tries to guess the number. "Number nine," she says, to a mixture of groans and cheers. In the "Monday Morning Means Math" quiz, Miss O'Brien randomly picks one math question before we start. If you get that question right you get a candy, even if you get all the other questions wrong. Everyone loves it.

We grab our pencils and math books. I try to catch Kyler's eye before Miss O'Brien gets started, but Kyler is a serious quiz-taker. His head is already down. Miss O'Brien launches straight into the questions. Now I'm going to have to tell him without making her nose quiver. This is not easy. Miss O'Brien's a great teacher, and she's really fun, but she can be strict too. She doesn't like anything messing up her Monday Morning Means Math quiz, that's for sure. The warning sign: she repeats herself for a second time, and then her nose begins to quiver.

As she turns to write on the board, I nudge Kyler. He shakes his head as if I'm a gnat buzzing around his ear.

"Kyler," I whisper. He swats me away. Five questions

later, I finally get his attention. He's ahead on the quiz and looking around to see how he's doing compared to everyone else. "I saw a Celtic warrior last night. A real Celt in the VA," I whisper.

Miss O'Brien looks around. Kyler makes a face. It's an "I don't believe you, and why don't you shut up before Miss O'Brien moves our behavior pegs to orange" kind of face.

"Mikey," Miss O'Brien points to my math book then returns to writing on the board.

I whisper again.

Miss O'Brien turns back to me. "Mikey, eyes on your work, please."

I try to tell Kyler one more time and Miss O'Brien twitches her nose. I shouldn't ignore the sign, but if I don't tell him now I'm going to burst. And then it's like some Celtic god has sent a thunderbolt from the sky. The classroom phone rings, and Miss O'Brien is distracted by someone in the office wanting to know whether Naomi Huang has gone to the dentist.

"He was up on one of those wheelie beds," I whisper. "Red hair, red mustache, torc, tattoos, ripping off his hospital gown, and yelling, 'Cuckoolaaand!'" I must have said that one word louder than I intended because all of a sudden Casey Rubens is singing, "Cuckooland, Cuckooland, Mikey's in cloud Cuckooland," in her chipmunk voice, and everyone's giggling and making whacko expressions at me.

Miss O'Brien puts the phone down. "What is going on? This is the Monday Morning Means Math quiz, and I should be able to talk on the telephone without pandemonium breaking loose. Pandemonium means lots of noise and goofing off."

She puts Casey's and my peg down to orange. Casey points at me as if it is my fault. I make a "too bad" face and shrug. I'm not worried. I'll get my peg back up again before the end of the day. She won't be so lucky. She never shuts up.

Kyler seems to get back to his math, but a few seconds later he nudges me and shows me the side of his scratch paper. *Red hair? Tattoos?* he writes. I nod crazily. *Ripped off his shirt? War cries??* He's really thinking it over now. *TORC????* I nod again.

No way, he writes.

Yes way, I write back. I grab a crayon from my pencil box and add some blood splatters and a puddle of red underneath to show I'm serious.

He thinks for a moment. I can tell he is thinking because his mouth hangs open, which is the way Kyler always thinks. Then he grins.

AWESOME!!!!!!!!!!! He writes exclamation marks across the page until his pencil lead breaks.

CHAPTER FOUR

At recess, I sit him down at one of the lunch tables, as far as we can get from other kids, and tell him everything while he pulls out his snacks. Kyler's the smallest, skinniest guy in our grade, but he's big on snacks.

"You should have seen him, Kyler. He was up on the bed, yelling, fierce as anything, and the look he had in his eyes…"

Kyler groans as if he's in pain and interrupts with stuff like, "I can't believe it. Why didn't Dad take me to the ER with you? This is killing me, Mikey, killing me!" But he doesn't doubt me, not once.

That's the great thing about Kyler. He's seen every time-travel documentary he can find, and he loves books where people are called "Zethos" and "Mildar" and live on planets where you can fall off the edge and every animal has two heads and six rows of teeth. So, a real live Celt in California doesn't come as too much of a shock.

I'm just getting to the truly amazing part, when Kyler interrupts. "So, he wore a torc and was covered in tattoos?"

"Yep," I say.

"And he freaked out, like he'd never seen modern stuff before—"

"That's it! So I took a picture to show you—"

"You got a picture?"

"No, but I tried, and that's when he pointed right at me. He spoke in a foreign language, and then he said, 'Not this time!' He knew he was in the wrong time, Kyler!"

"Wow!" Kyler throws his arms back and splays his legs out, as if he's just collapsed. "Wow," he says again.

"I know!" I feel myself break into an emoticon grin. Life doesn't get any better than this. "So, I guess he'd just traveled here, or got transported or whatever, which is why he was freaking out—"

"But he spoke English," Kyler says, pulling a chocolate milk from his bag.

"And another language, too."

"Yeah, but he spoke English and the Celts didn't."

I can't believe Kyler's worrying about this right now. "So, the guy was speaking English. So what?"

"So…if he's learned some English…then he must have been here for a long time or maybe it's not the first time he's traveled here?"

"Oh man, you're right, that's kind of what your mom said."

"Mom?" Kyler sits bolt upright. "My mom was there? In the room?"

"Yeah, didn't I say?" I feel kind of sick. I can't make myself look Kyler in the face, so I look at the ground instead. It feels awkward, but it's a lot less awkward than telling Kyler I think his mom is part of a conspiracy to hush up time travel. Doesn't that make her a bad guy? "She was awesome, by the way," I mumble.

"So? What did she say?"

There's something about direct questions that I hate. I think it's that millisecond of thinking I could lie and then knowing I can't. "She took me aside, Kyler. Told me it was a big secret, but it's been happening for years." Just saying it out loud makes my voice crack with the sense of how awesome this is. "They come on certain nights. He's not the only one, and sometimes the same guys keep coming back."

"Wow!" Kyler leans forward and shakes his head. "So, you think this guy has been here before and that my mom is…like…in on it?"

"I don't know," I say, because I really don't. "When I called him a Celt, she acted shocked. She tried to laugh it off, but she couldn't. Then she got real serious and said it was against the rules to tell me about him. That's what she said. 'Against the rules.'"

There's a moment of silence and then Kyler leaps up. "Coooooool!" he shouts, as if I just made his day. I may have been worried about casting his mom as a mad scientist, but he sure isn't.

He throws his hand up for a high five, does an "oh yeah" dance and, when he spills his chocolate milk, just laughs as it puddles around his feet. That's how happy he is. "It's a conspiracy! Just like the documentaries online. The VA is transporting warriors from ancient times as part of a secret defense project, to study them—"

"Or use them as secret weapons," I say.

"Yeah, and I bet there's a time travel machine in the basement of the VA and doctors, like Mom, have to look after the warriors because, well, who knows what time travel will do to a guy? So totally cool!"

I knew Kyler would get it. "Cool? It's not just cool. It's awesome. It's unreal!" I say.

"No, Mikey, this is real." Kyler drops his voice. He looks really serious. "Wood frogs in Alaska freeze themselves solid for seven months of the year. If you pick one up and bend its leg, it'll break off, but in the summer that frog will thaw out, hop around—"

"Not if you break its leg off," I say.

He waves my comment away. "That frog will be fine, until next winter when it freezes again. I mean, who would believe that? But it's true." I love it when Kyler's like this. "And dinosaurs, who would believe them, really? Or kissing. Like that's really weird, but it happens."

"Gross!"

"Just saying!" He flops back on the bench, rips open a bag of seaweed rice crackers, and offers me one. I crunch down a few times and realize that something doesn't add up. Something about Kyler's totally amazing theory, and my conversation with Mariko, doesn't work.

"But your mom didn't know who was arriving, or when. She just said certain nights they came. She wasn't expecting them." I sit next to him. "Dude, if the VA doctors were in on the project, wouldn't they be told when to expect these guys?" Kyler doesn't answer, but his mouth drops open in "Kyler thinking" mode. "And, wouldn't the Defense Department have a secure facility, miles away from anywhere, so the time-traveled warriors couldn't escape right away?" I'm thinking of the secret Area 51 base where they built the stealth airplanes. If they did that in the 1970s, wouldn't they do the same for this, now?

"Maybe he escaped?"

"Then they need to up their security big time, because your mom's seen men like the Celt before. They can't all be escaping. The Defense Department wouldn't set up a project this humongous and then be so bad at protecting it." I grab for Kyler's rice crackers and throw a whole handful in my mouth before he can pull the bag away. I have this theory that eating something crunchy stimulates the brain. The popping noise gets the neurons, or whatever they're called, popping too. Worked for me once on my nine times table. I memorized it by synchronizing my thoughts to the crunches. I've sworn by it ever since. So I crunch away.

When the idea comes, it's so obvious I stand up as if electrified. "It's not organized, Kyler. It's just happening. There's more activity on certain nights, that's what your mom said. Nights when bad things are happening, natural disasters and stuff, but the VA doesn't know when that is. All they know is they get these guys, they treat some of them, some disappear back to wherever, and some return again."

"But, then what are they doing here?"

I shrug. "I don't know, but the VA and the government obviously know about it. The weird thing is they're keeping it secret, but they're still letting it happen. Why would they do that?"

"Because they can't control it?" Kyler makes a "what do you think?" stretchy face, his mouth turned down. "Maybe it's some kind of crazy natural phenomenon?"

"And that's why they have to keep it secret!" All that research last night is paying off. "Time travel is the biggest military weapon a country could ever invent!" I'm trembling as I say it. "Travel back in time and you can change whatever you want. You can control the entire history of the world. If the government knows there's some weird "natural time travel" thing going on, they aren't going to let anyone else know until they understand it and control it themselves. They're definitely not going to let other countries—or terrorists—know."

I pause for a moment and I see the Celt clearly again, in that moment before the nurses gathered around, his blue eyes not fierce anymore, but sad. "'I don't want to get stuck here.'"

"Say again."

"That's what he said. 'I don't want to get stuck here.' It makes total sense. Maybe he's afraid he'll never get back to the portal or time machine or whatever he has to use to return home. He'll be stuck in this time, forever!"

Kyler thumps his fist on the table. "Why didn't I think of this?" he says. I guess he's bummed about me trashing his theory. I'm going to tell him not to take it so hard. Kyler's real smart normally, and he can be hard on himself, but then he leans in and whispers, "I heard Mom talking to Dad this morning when she got off her shift."

"And?"

"Well…" He holds on to the word for a really long time just to bug me.

"What?"

"She said a patient ran away last night."

"No!"

"Yeah, a patient ran away."

I grab Kyler's shoulders and pretty much shake his head off in time with my words. "It's him. It must be him. That proves it! He's gonna try to get back to his own time. We have to find him, see it with our own eyes. This is probably our only chance, ever, to prove that time travel really exists!"

CHAPTER FIVE

Romanii: Northern Borders has never felt so real as it does tonight. These guys aren't just computer-generated anymore. I've seen a Celtic warrior. I've heard him. I've smelled him. I've even spoken to him. I should be relishing every moment of my epic victory against the Romans, but I can hardly concentrate. "Let's pause," I whisper.

I have to repeat myself twice before Kyler finally understands. "Good call!" he whispers back with a thumbs-up. It's always risky playing *Romanii* during the week. We have to keep our voices especially low. Even if Mom is working the night shift, Grandpa is still under strict instructions to close me down. No war games during the week, only four hours max on the weekend. That's why Grandpa's monthly poker nights are so great.

"I can't think of anything but the Celt. The real Celt!" I say.

"Me too. Let's get back to planning. We have to have a plan."

"I know, but what? He's run away. He could be anywhere. Did you ask your mom whether they'd found him again?"

"Yeah, I slipped her the question on the way back from my violin lesson. She'd totally forgotten it was Dad she was talking to about him, not me. The Celt has disappeared, for sure."

"Good, that's easier for us."

"Easier?" Kyler does a giant "what do you mean" face into the screen, which makes me laugh.

"We know he's still out there. It's easier for us to find him outside than in the VA with all those doctors around all the time."

Kyler shrugs. "I could just pretend I was visiting Mom," he mumbles. "Anyway how do we know he hasn't already gone back to his own time?"

"We don't," I say, "but we've got to start somewhere. We have to assume he's still here and find him before he goes back." Kyler's looking pretty unhappy about the whole situation, like he wants to give up. Well, no way! No way are we giving up on this.

I grab my military history book and hold the cover up to the screen. "For inspiration," I say. Kyler holds up some chips. It's a good idea. I take a few from the bag Grandpa let me have from his poker store and crunch. They were supposed to help me with my homework, but I figure I am at home and I'm thinking, so this is like homework.

"OK, so, you're a Celt, and you've time-traveled to the future. What would you do?" I flip some pages, looking at the pictures.

Kyler blows air through his lips and lifts his shoulders to his ears. "I dunno. Go get ice cream? Fly around the world? All the stuff I couldn't do back in my time?"

"Kyler," I groan. "He was freaked out."

"OK, then I'd hide."

"Right. He's going to lay low someplace until he can get back to his own time again."

"So, where do you think he is?"

I'm looking at a page about Celtic weapons and how the Celts offered swords to the gods. It talks about the druids and their sacred oak groves. An idea comes. I wait a couple of seconds to let Kyler anticipate my genius. "In a park," I say.

Kyler snorts as if he's not that impressed.

"No, listen. It makes sense. The Celts hated towns. They conquered Rome. Rome, Kyler! It didn't get any better than that, and you know what? They left again. They didn't want to live there. Celts were into wild places. They worshipped oak trees, and they left offerings for their gods in ponds and marshes. If I were this guy, I'd hide somewhere I felt safe."

Kyler puts his head to one side. His jaw drops open.

"Got a better idea?" I say.

"No," Kyler says slowly. "That's good, Mikey. That's pretty good."

"So here's how we start. We check out a different park every day when we walk to school. We can do it without our moms—without anyone—knowing. If you print out a map tonight, we can make our first trip tomorrow. Meanwhile, I'll do more reading about Celts and see if I can find any other clues."

Kyler still looks unconvinced, so I try to pump him up.

"Look, it's a special mission. We'll call it Operation Celt." Kyler makes a face. "OK. Operation…" I crunch one more chip. "Operation Vercingetorix!"

"What did you say?"

"Where…kin…get...uh…rix. He was a Gaul, a French Celt, who led a revolt against Julius Caesar."

"Seriously?"

"Yes! Where…kin…get...uh…rix. At least, that's how Dad says it, and he took Latin in school."

"Wow. Cool. Operation Vercingetorix."

"Or Operation Where Can Get a Celt." I start to giggle. "Instead of get…uh…rix!"

"Operation Getaceltorix." Kyler wants to shout, I can tell, but he can't so he does a sort of crazy whisper instead, contorting his lips as he speaks.

"You're one scary dude!" I say.

Kyler gives me a double thumbs-up.

I do the same.

"Operation Getaceltorix! The hunt is on!"

CHAPTER SIX

The next morning, Kyler's at my house extra early with a map he's printed off the Internet. "Got it," he shouts, waving the paper in my face before I can shut him up.

"What's that, Kyler?" Mom raises her eyebrows as she sweeps veggie peelings into the trash. I should have warned Kyler she'd be here this morning. She has a sixth sense for trouble.

When she's not on nights, Mom likes to get up and make sure I eat a good breakfast. Cooked stuff. "Protein not pastries," she always says. She packs my lunch box, too, with salads, fruit, and carrot sticks. On these mornings, Grandpa stays in bed with his cup of coffee. "To keep it company," he says, but he's really keeping out of Mom's way.

When it's just Grandpa and me, I eat a huge bowl of cereal for breakfast. Without milk. The crunching sets me up for the day brainwise. Then Grandpa makes me a chocolate-spread sandwich the size of my military history book for lunch, and I grab a bag of chips from his poker night store hidden in the garage. Grandpa's packed lunches are great. Mom disagrees. I've tried telling her chips are brain food, but she's not bought into this yet.

"Carrots are crunchier…and nutritious!" She sounds like a health food commercial.

Anyway, the minute Kyler sees Mom in the kitchen he looks guilty. He hides the map behind his back and squeaks hello. Wrong move. Mom leans over the counter with a look that says she knows something's up.

"The map! Great," I say, quickly. "Miss O'Brien will give us extra credit, for sure."

Mom chops an apple, eyebrows still raised. "Are you two working on something for school?"

Kyler nods and glances at me. I want to cover for him, but why does he leave the direct question to me? He should know by now they aren't my strong suit.

Mom asks again, "Is that something for school?"

No, I want to say, we're looking for a Celtic warrior in every park we can find. "No," I find myself saying, "I mean, yeah." I hesitate. "It's a map of our route to school," which is true. "And we want to work on it a bit more before class."

"Great," Mom says. "Is Miss O'—" She glances at the clock. "Oh! My goodness, look at the time. I have a dentist appointment in twenty minutes, and I haven't finished your fruit salad yet. Mikey, go brush your teeth."

We're saved! Kyler and I run upstairs like we have

rocket packs strapped to our backs.

"Lucky," Kyler says as he slams my bedroom door. He puts the map on my desk and points with a pencil as he talks. "Now listen up." Kyler can take stuff really seriously sometimes, but that's OK. I'm glad he's with me on this. "There are five parks in town. Only two are within walking distance of school. So, those are the ones we'll try first. We'll call them Park One and Park Two. And there are grounds around the VA, which we'll consider Park Three. Parks Four and Five we'll have to get someone to drive us, so let's forget them for now."

"He won't have stayed at the VA last night. The police will have searched all around it."

"Agreed…so let's start at Park One, the farthest away, walking-distance-wise." Kyler circles Park One on the map.

"Hey, isn't that 'Big Stick Park' right by our old preschool? That's what I used to call it. It has those great trees along the fence, with the best sticks ever, and that cool digger thing in the sandbox?" Kyler looks blank. "You lost a tooth there when you fell off the swing set."

"You mean 'Lost Tooth Park'?" He shudders. "I hate that park."

"That reminds me…" I run to the bathroom and rub some toothpaste onto my front teeth.

When I come back I notice Kyler has drawn a sad

face on Park One, and colored our new route to school in red.

"Hey," he says, "I was thinking, have you looked in the flour canister?"

"What for? The Celt?" I grab the map.

"Duh, no. The guns? They could be in a plastic snack bag, taped to the bottom?" It sounds insane, but I know exactly what he means.

"Already looked," I say. "Come on, there's no time to think about Mom's plastic-gun stash right now." We head for the stairs.

Grandpa meets us on the landing as he comes out of his bedroom. "Have you brushed your teeth?" he asks. He's wearing his grandpa-grey robe with an empty coffee cup tied to the flannel belt. This drives Mom mad, but Grandpa says it frees up his hands, and she'd be even madder if he fell down the stairs. A small trickle of coffee dribbles onto the floor. "Have a nice day, Mikey Boy. Kyler too. Don't forget to show those teachers how smart you are, just in case they haven't noticed. Heh, heh." Grandpa presses chocolate-covered peppermints, his favorite candy, into our hands.

"Thanks, Grandpa," I say. "See you later."

As we're hurrying out the door, Mom holds me back to stuff my lunch box into my backpack. I breathe toothpaste on her. She seems convinced, because she wishes me goodbye and gives me a kiss.

The minute the door's closed, Kyler and I leap down the front steps. "One Mississippi, two Mississippi, go, go, go!" We're special operations paratroopers launching out of our troop plane on our first mission of the day.

"Operation Getaceltorix here we go!" I yell. We land, throw a pretend roll, then high five each other as we step into the heavy morning mist. I know it's unlikely we'll find him on the first day, especially since it's October thirteenth, which is not a lucky day if you believe those things, but it sure feels good to be looking.

Our "mom-approved" route to school is straight down the street one block, left three blocks, then right two blocks. Even so, it took until fourth grade for Mom to let me walk there alone. Now I can, as long as I take my phone, but she's happier when Kyler's with me. She used to spy on us, I'm sure: driving past to watch whether we crossed the street properly. But she's finally gotten over that. Still, as we turn at the first block and then turn right—completely off our mom-approved route—I'm thinking she'll be really mad, grounding mad, no-TV-for-a-month mad, if she finds out about this. Better keep on the alert.

"Corporal Kyler, take point and keep your eyes peeled. We may be watched," I say in my walkie-talkie voice, adding a bit of static for effect. "Kechhhhh. The target could be anywhere. He may be armed and dangerous. Kechhhhh. Out."

"Roger," Kyler says. "Kechhhh. Out." Kyler steps ahead of me to become the lookout, while I spin to cover our rear.

We walk the whole way like this, Kyler checking the map at every cross street, me walking backwards to make sure we aren't ambushed. We're pretty much there when I hear Kyler say, "Butt."

This is one of our games. I'm not sure it fits into Operation Getaceltorix, but I go along with it and say, "Butt cheek." I wait for Kyler's reply. He's supposed to say, "Butt cheek cooties," or something like that. The aim is to keep adding words until the other guy laughs, but Kyler doesn't add anything. I shout, "Butt cheek," again as loud as I can and run into Kyler's back. I look around to see what's stopped him in his tracks.

Ryan O'Driscoll is coming out of the park right in front of us. Kyler tugs at my sleeve, but it's too late. I've just shouted, "Butt cheek," at Ryan O'Driscoll.

Ryan's the biggest guy in fourth grade. It's not just that he's tall. He's the kid version of a muscle car. He always wears long basketball shorts, and his calves bulge like the turkey legs they sell at county fairs. Fog is still hanging in damp pockets in the hollows of the road, but Ryan is in a short-sleeved basketball shirt, and he hasn't got one goose bump. He's carrying a camouflage backpack like mine and has stars and stripes shaved into his crew cut. Mom always tuts disapprovingly when she sees this. "When you're ten years old, you should be a kid not a fashion statement," she says, but Kyler and I think his haircut is cool. Our moms would never let us have a cut like that in a million years.

"What did you say?" Ryan asks, blocking our way. I'm never putting Kyler on point again. He's supposed to look out for danger not walk into it. "What're you doing here?"

Oh man, this is Ryan all over. In second grade he was fun. We were never good enough friends to go play at his house, but Ryan was a building-brick genius and recess champion at "Squash the Tofu," a game I made up. Now he just gets mean and moody. I'm not saying Ryan's a bully. He doesn't normally pick on people. It's just that you never know nowadays when he's going to lose it. Like, he drops the ball in Squash the Tofu, or someone piles on his head, which is half the fun, and he gets red-faced mad really quickly. Just like he's doing right this minute.

"What're you doing in my park?" he says again.

It's a direct question darn it, and I can feel the words forming on the end of my tongue.

"Looking for a—"

Kyler cuts in for once. "It's not your park. It's every-one's. What are you doing?"

Ryan looks surprised then says, "Going for a run, Turtle."

I groan a double groan. Kyler hates being called "Turtle," even though he does look like one because he's so small and his backpack is so big. And I'm so not surprised Ryan O'Driscoll is running while wearing a backpack. He's probably doing pull-ups every morning and a hundred one-armed push-ups, too.

"You're jogging?" Kyler says. "Jogging what? Your brains into jelly?"

"Kyler!" I go to pull him away, but it's too late. Ryan takes a swing. Kyler ducks. I step to one side. Ryan swings at me, too. I run. "Come on!"

Kyler follows me back up the street with Ryan thumping along behind us.

"You've done it now," I shout, wondering if we can outrun him, and, even if we do, what he'll be like at school after this. Calling Ryan "Butt Cheek" and insult-ing his brainpower is not a good way to start the day.

Maybe we slow down around the corner without realizing it, because one minute we're sprinting away from Ryan, up a small street with a laundromat and a grocery store, and the next minute he's right up close. "Are you spying on me, Turtle?"

I glance over my shoulder to see Ryan yanking at a loose strap hanging from Kyler's backpack. Kyler spins around on the sidewalk. His arms flail above his head as he wobbles into the gutter. Ryan loosens his grip for a second. I shout, "Run!" like Kyler doesn't know that already, and then Ryan clamps down on Kyler's arm.

It all happens so quickly. Ryan wrestles Kyler to the ground. I see panic on Kyler's face and I wade in to help just as there's a roar from the alley between the store and the laundromat. All the garbage cans rattle. A cloud of warm steam streams out of the dryer exhausts. A black cat runs down the street hissing. And a man, as big as a bear, leaps out of the fog yelling, "Cuckoolaaand!"

It's my warrior with his clumpy red hair and his mustache dripping fog. Spit sprays out of his mouth in a big arc like a lawn sprinkler. Whoa. He's every bit as amazing as in the VA, but more scary. Way more scary because he's outside, on his own, with no adults around to help, and he's mad at us. Like really mad. And suddenly, even though we came looking for him, I am terrified.

CHAPTER SEVEN

Ryan launches forward as if he's going to attack the guy. I can't believe it. What's he thinking? Fighting a Celt? He'll be torn apart!

"Stop!" I thrust my whole body sideways into Ryan, pushing him out of the way, so I can put myself in front of the Celt. I hold both my hands out as if I'm stopping traffic. "I was at the VA. I'm a friend." Crud, I hope he remembers or he's going to cream me.

The Celt staggers back as if he's more surprised than I am. Then Ryan's stumbling over to the wall of the laundromat, sobbing, "No! Just go!" His nose is running snot. I don't know whether he's talking to us or to the Celt, but I don't get the chance to find out because Kyler's dragging me along the sidewalk, yelling, "Come on!"

"Wait!" I try to shake Kyler's grip, all the while twisting to keep the Celt in sight. "It's OK, he's a friend," I cry, but Kyler's got momentum and, although he's small, he's impossible to fight off.

"Geez," he keeps saying, over and over, "geez." He's already pulled me past the laundromat when I finally decide to sit down in the gutter. That stops him. Kyler loses his balance and falls back into me.

"Quit pulling me. That's him!" I say.

"What?"

"We found him, on the very first day!" I slap the sidewalk with my hand.

"Oh man! I was so freaked, and now we're gonna lose him again—where did he go?"

"Down the—"

I don't have time to finish my sentence. Kyler's on his feet and we're both running toward the laundromat and its clouds of steam. Ryan's collapsed against the wall by the front door, one shoulder leaning against it, his legs spaghetti twisted, as he stares down the alley. He's weirded out, I guess, because he's as pale as noodles and shaking. As I run past, he turns his face into the bricks.

"Sorry, Ryan," I mutter. Ryan doesn't say a thing.

Because of the dryer exhausts, the alley feels twenty degrees warmer than the street, even though the sun hasn't risen high enough to peek down here yet. It's all fog, trash, and grafitti. There are detergent boxes spilling out of trash bags next to the back door of the laundromat, and a bunch of grocery cartons from the store with chip and beef jerky logos on them.

"Can you see him?" Kyler whispers.

"No." I creep along, weaving between the dumpsters.

Kyler follows.

"We really shouldn't be doing this," he whispers, and he's right. Mom will kill me if she finds out. Big time screen ban. No TV, minimum. But this is a Celt we're talking about.

Behind the dumpsters, people have laid sheets of cardboard to sleep on. There are blankets too, dirty coats and plastic bags piled high against the grimy black walls. Torn strips of paper and cardboard stick to the ground in dirty brown wads, reminding me of the collages Kyler's little brother makes. They always end up brown. There are puddles of dark water in every dip in the bricks, and the alley smells of pee.

Kyler overtakes me, hurrying to look behind the final cluster of garbage cans, about three quarters of the way down. My heart slams a few extra beats when he sticks his head up.

"Found him?" I call.

Kyler shakes his head. "He's gone!"

I catch up with him. He's right. The Celt is nowhere to be seen.

"It's all my fault," Kyler groans. "That was insane. Never saw anyone so scary in my life. But he was just like you said, Mikey. A Celt! Awesome!"

"Awesome," I agree. "But where did he go?"

"I don't know."

We high five in the dark stink of the alley because even though we've lost him this time, we have a real live Celtic warrior in our town. A shiver runs down my back. It's only when we walk a few extra feet and we're out on the other side of the alley that we start to laugh.

"You should have seen your face," I say. The smell of fresh hot doughnuts drifts across the street. My mouth waters, and I feel good again right away. I push Kyler, and he pushes me back.

"Did you see Ryan's face? He looked like he'd seen a ghost," Kyler says.

"He saw our Celt. A real time-traveled Celt! That's better than a ghost."

Then Kyler throws himself against the door of a store and blubs, "No, just go!" It's a pretty bad imitation of Ryan, but I know what he means, and we double over laughing. When I look up trying to catch my breath, I catch sight of the clock in the doughnut shop.

"We are so late!" I adjust my backpack.

"Oh no, just go!" Kyler flings his arms in the air and fake sobs again. He wants us to keep laughing, but we've got to hurry. I start back down the alley, but it feels too creepy, so we end up running down the street we're already on. At the intersection, we join up with the red route we planned this morning.

"He just appeared…" Kyler shouts as he runs beside

me, "in all that fog and steam, and then disappeared again. Like magic."

"Not science?" I ask, thinking how much Kyler loves his physics.

"Maybe science and magic are the same thing…if you're a Celt."

I hadn't thought of it like that, but now that Kyler says it I can't help wondering if it's true. This is the greatest thing ever. First day, and we found him. No. Even more spooky, he found us. "He remembered me. He protected us from Ryan." I'm gasping for breath now as we get near school. "How did he even know where we were?"

"Maybe he's following us?"

"You think?"

"You said it yourself, Mikey, you're his only friend. Maybe he needs help? We've got to be open to all possibilities," Kyler says. "We have to be governed by the evidence." Kyler can run and say "governed by the evidence," without panting. That's a brown belt for you.

The school bell goes off. The last three tetherball guys slide into their classrooms. We're still way over on the other side of the blacktop, officially late, but I don't care.

"We've found a Celtic warrior!" I yell to Kyler.

"This is the best day ever!" Kyler shouts back.

"Epic!" And it doesn't even occur to me to worry about leaving Ryan behind.

CHAPTER EIGHT

Miss O'Brien's already finishing roll call when we hit the classroom. I manage to get my backpack in my cubby and sit down before she calls me. That's one good thing about having a last name near the end of the alphabet. Kyler's name has already been called out. She waits until she's called everyone else before she goes back to him. She gives us a look. I'm sure she's going to send us to the office. Then I notice Sawyer Bradstone isn't here yet. *Thank you, Sawyer.* He's always late. He doesn't come in for another ten minutes, which makes us look like angels.

Miss O'Brien isn't mad when Sawyer arrives, but she makes him go to the office because she's already emailed her class numbers.

"What was it today, Sawyer?" she asks when he gets back. He's got a huge smile on his face, and we all know we're in for a story.

"Justine pooped right when Mom was buckling her in. It squirted down her leg and all over the car seat. Massive pool of yellow poop."

"Ewwwww!" The whole class groans. A few kids hold

their noses and pretend to gag. Babies are gross like that, especially Sawyer's new twin sisters.

"Thank you, class," Miss O'Brien says. "Your mom did well to get you here at all, Sawyer. Twins are hard work."

I think Miss O'Brien knows when Sawyer's going to gross us out, and she lets him speak anyway. It brightens our day. Miss O'Brien likes us laughing, as long as we're not too wild.

It's only after we get started on Language Arts, which I dread, that I wonder about Ryan. He's not here yet. I pass Kyler a note. *Where's Ryan?* I write.

Kyler replies with *"Oooooh, nooooo, just goooooo!"* in jiggly writing that would be squeaky if it could speak.

The rest of the lesson Kyler keeps his head down over his work. He fills in his worksheet in double-quick time, which means he has time to do the harder worksheet for "fun." The annoying thing is, he does seem to find it fun. It takes me nearly the whole class to do the first one, so I only have a few minutes to think about how amazing it was to find the Celt…or for him to find us, as Kyler suggested. That gets me thinking. Kyler said something about science and magic…magic and science. The idea plays around in my head. I remember some of the sidebars in my military history book about how the Celts didn't believe in death, which is what made them so scary on the battlefield, and I don't have to crunch anything. My neurons are popping on their own today! I draw a jack-o'-lantern on my scratch paper. It has the biggest grin ever because that's how I'm feeling right now.

When Miss O'Brien lets us out for recess, I can hardly wait for Kyler to find his snack bag. "Come on, Kyler, let's go to the bushes. I have an idea."

We're running across the blacktop with Kyler fake-swinging his snack bag at me when we notice a whole group of kids clustered around a boy from another class. He's talking loudly and looking toward the school office, saying something like, "The guy was freaked!" We exchange glances and run over to listen.

"No seriously, Ryan O'Driscoll was attacked! Guy jumped out at him from an alley."

"How do you know?" someone asks.

"I told you, he was in the office when I went for a bandage."

"Did he get mugged?"

"No, but the lady from the laundromat found him. She said he refused to go home, so she brought him to school."

"He wanted to come to school instead of going home? That's weird," another kid jokes.

"I heard them talking. Then they sent him to see Miss Wendy."

Miss Wendy is the school counselor. She comes into

our class to talk about bullying and being fair on the playground, things like that. Kyler nudges me. We make for the bushes, but some other kids have already snagged them, so we hide behind the Lost and Found rack instead.

"What are we gonna do?" he says. "Do you think the laundromat lady saw us, too? Do you think Ryan'll say we were with him?"

"If he does, our moms will find out we were on the wrong street, not the mom-approved route. They'll be really mad," I say. We look at each other.

"What can we do?" Kyler asks.

I shrug. "I suppose we should come clean and tell Miss Wendy we saw everything. But we'll be in real trouble. We shouldn't have left Ryan behind."

Kyler ignores my last comment. "Tell Miss Wendy about our Celt? No way!"

"Keep your voice down. He's our secret. Remember? No one knows except us."

"And Ryan," Kyler says.

"Ryan *saw* him, but he doesn't know he's a Celt. Only we know that. Even you didn't recognize him at first."

"Don't remind me. I totally blew it." Kyler hammers on his head with a fist. "I'm so dumb. We had the chance to talk to him, actually talk to him, and find out how this whole thing works, and I ran away. If he's gone back to his own time now, I'll—"

"Maybe he can't get back yet," I interrupt, feeling myself grin like a dopey dog while I wait for Kyler's reaction.

"What do you mean?"

"You said science and magic were the same thing for Celts." Kyler looks a bit surprised, like he can't even remember saying that. "Pure genius! I did some reading last night, and, get this, the Celts believed in a place called the Otherworld."

"What's that?"

"The place you went when you died."

"So you think our Celt is a *ghost*?" Kyler waits a second. "Then Ryan was right to go white when he saw him!"

I can tell he's about to do another imitation of Ryan. I shut him up quick. "No, he's not a ghost. I saw him in the ER. Ghosts can't have IVs stuck in them. But Celts weren't ghosts when they were in the Otherworld. You still had a body. It was just like earth, except better. You stayed there until you died in the Otherworld. Then you were reborn on earth again. Then you died on earth—"

"OK, I get it. You had a yo-yo body and soul." Kyler really surprises me sometimes.

"Yeah! Totally, and that's why the Celts were so scary. They didn't believe in death. They knew they would live in the Otherworld and return to earth, often with other people they knew, time and time again."

Kyler wobbles his head. "Hippy," he says. "But what's that got to do with anything?"

"You didn't have to be dead to get to the Otherworld, either. There were times and places when the skin between the Otherworld and this world was thin. People could cross between them in special places like lakes and rivers —wet places, foggy places. Celts were big into fog."

"But we aren't near a lake or a river."

"The Celt appeared near a laundromat, Kyler. Think about it. Lots of water in a laundromat."

"You have to be kidding."

"Times change. And there was fog," I say. "Tons of fog this morning, and all those dryer exhausts."

By the look on his face, Kyler's not buying it. So I reach for the big guns. "And if a living person crossed into the Otherworld, they could live there for what seemed like a day, but when they crossed back to their normal lives something like five hundred years could have gone by."

That's when Kyler starts hopping from one foot to the other in excitement. "Seriously? He could have crossed into the Otherworld, in his time, and walked out again sometime way, way, in the future…like now?"

"You got it!" I say. "It's the Celtic version of time travel! And that's why he was saying: 'Not this time!' He probably only went to the Otherworld for an hour or two and now he's freaking out because he's left all his family behind. He doesn't want to be here, Kyler. He wants to get back home, to his time!"

Suddenly Kyler's scrabbling in his snack bag, in his pockets and, in desperation, in the pockets of the coats hanging on the Lost and Found rack. "Pencil," he gasps. "Paper!"

I have a piece of paper stuffed in my pocket. The Lost and Found donates a ballpoint. Kyler grabs them both, folds the paper in two and then stabs the ballpoint right through. "I'm thinking 'wormholes,' Mikey. Celtic wormholes through time!"

The minute he says this, I remember one of our time-travel videos. "A wormhole is a time tunnel through space, but the Otherworld is a Celtic tunnel between different times on earth!"

"That's it! Imagine this ballpoint is a tunnel. We've just found a shortcut from this side of the paper," Kyler points to the top, "to this side." He points to the bottom. "Or from this time," he traces his finger around the entire curve of the paper, "to this time. That's a wormhole. The Otherworld is a wormhole. You go into it in, say, 410 A.D. and you come out in 2010 A.D." Then he does a kind of "ta-da" step. "Maybe the Celts were quantum physicists."

"But with bigger mustaches!" I say. I have to give it to

Kyler. He's always been a smart guy. If he ate chips, like me, every time he read a book, he'd be a super brain by now—fat, sure, but real brainy. We're about to high five when Kyler pulls his hand away.

"We know how he's time traveling. He's going into the Otherworld wormhole and coming out the other side. So, is the alley one of those foggy crossing places, like a magic portal?"

"Yeah, that's it!"

"But can he control it?"

I think about this really carefully, trying to remember exactly what he looked like in the hospital and what he said. "No, I don't think so. He said, 'Not this time,' like it was a mistake that he's made before and he didn't want to make it again."

"So did we just see him leave for good this morning when he disappeared? Maybe he got lucky this time and got back home?" Kyler looks up at the sky with his hands clasped as if he's begging the Celtic gods. "Please don't let that be true!"

"That's what I was trying to tell you," I say as the bell rings for the end of recess.

Kyler groans with frustration as he pushes out from behind the Lost and Found rack and starts running across the blacktop. "What?"

I follow him. "The key is 'certain nights'. Your mom

said the men came on certain nights. That's all we know." I stop for a moment. "But it makes perfect sense. The Celts believed there were certain nights when the skin between the Otherworld and this world was thin. The very best night was Halloween! I bet he's stuck here until Halloween. We have to keep looking for him."

"That's what I needed to hear!" Kyler cheers. "Operation Getaceltorix worked this morning. It'll work again tomorrow. Same time, same route," he says as we sprint to class.

"If we gain his trust, maybe he'll even take us with him," I say.

Kyler whoops in agreement. "He'll show us his horses, his chariot, everything."

I hurl a pretend spear at our classroom door. "And we'll fight alongside him. We'll be warriors!"

CHAPTER NINE

I'm glaring at a yellow college pad, trying to write a book report before dinner. So far I've written one sentence about ten times, on ten different pieces of paper, which are now in the trash. I keep thinking about the Celt. Grandpa always says you mustn't wish your life away, but I can't wait to look for him tomorrow. Somehow Kyler and I have to get back to the alley.

I text Kyler.

> What time tomorrow?

Kyler doesn't answer.

I lean over a new piece of paper, trying to concentrate on my report, but the page stays blank.

I text again.

> What do we tell moms?
> Reason 4 leaving 4 school
> early 2x this week is…?

Still no answer. Why doesn't Kyler check his phone? I work some more on my report. I get a couple of good smears of ink on there, squeeze out the first sentence again, and then a couple more.

I text Kyler to see if he wants to carry on our battle in *Romanii: Northern Borders*. We've been so busy we haven't had the chance to finish it yet. When he doesn't reply this time, I text:

> Afraid I'm going to whoop
> your butt?

Then I remember he has Tae Kwon Do. That's why he's not near his phone. I bet he's already finished his book report, too.

Kyler finds schoolwork easy. I watch him write sometimes, like when he was doing his worksheet today. All those words and ideas just flow out of him. He never seems to forget what he was saying at the start of the sentence, never sits there with the words coming out in the wrong order or not coming out at all.

I look back at my paper. I've read the book. I like reading books. I just hate writing about them. I straighten up to think, lean back over, and push my pen across the paper. One more sentence, two more, then I get stuck on a spelling. I cross the word out. Try again. Write it out a third time—and by then I've forgotten what I was trying to say. The page looks a mess. Mom would tell me to copy it out again, but I need a break.

I throw the pen down and delve into the box of building bricks by my desk. Just the sound of the plastic bricks rattling makes me relax. I picture the whole scene I want to make: a Roman city with walls around it, a forum in the middle, and streets in a grid pattern. Then I'm going to have my Celts ransack it, just like the real Celts did early in Rome's history. Maybe my Celt was there? He could have been.

I dig further through my storage boxes for some of the big baseplates to build on. These days, I like playing *Romanii: Northern Borders* best, but sometimes it's good to go "old style." I used to create giant battle scenes across my bedroom floor, and then my plastic soldiers would go to war. I still have them—hundreds of soldiers from different ages, Romans, Celts, Egyptians, Vikings, redcoats, pirates, Civil-War guys, D-Day-landing dudes—but the funny thing is, I have no guns. It's a Mom thing.

When I was little, every birthday I'd ask for soldiers. After a while she gave in and bought them for me, but even though they should have had guns, they never did. It took me years to figure out that Mom opened each set, took out the tiny guns, and resealed it before she gave it to me. She'd even black out the pictures of the guns on the outside of the box with a marker.

So I have this idea that she's hidden them. Somewhere

in this house there's an arsenal of miniature weaponry of epic proportions, and I'm going to find it. I look sometimes, on nights when she's working. It sounds crazy, I guess, but Kyler agrees with me. Knowing Mom, she's kept the guns because she sure as heck has kept all the boxes. One day she plans to sell everything online. She's told me. "Toys always get more if you still have the boxes, the instructions, and all the pieces," she said.

Kyler loves this whole "mini-weapons dump" idea. That's why, at the most unexpected times, he'll say "plastic bag, bottom of coffee can," or "scooped-out spaghetti squash, back of the kitchen cupboard." It's become another of our games, and some of his ideas are pretty good.

Anyway, I borrow a whole lot of pale green and ivory bricks from my castle set and a bunch of white bricks from my spaceships. There was a lot of marble and fancy decoration in Rome. It's already looking good when Mom calls me into the kitchen.

"Mikey, dinner for you and Grandpa is in the slow cooker. Set the table. Grandpa will serve."

She's about to go to work. She's wearing her uniform, and she's stuffing herself with salad in front of her laptop, emailing Dad before her shift. I tell her to say hi to Dad for me. She's got her commuter cup of coffee ready for the drive. I can tell she's already drunk half of it. She'll have to pour herself another before she leaves.

"Dad, can you turn the TV down?" she calls. "I need to talk to Mikey."

My heart freezes. Ryan's said something.

I glance into the living room. Grandpa's in his chair watching the news. He fumbles around on a little table next to him for the remote.

"Just doing it. Now where is that…?"

Mom sighs. "Get it for him, Mikey." She hates the new giant flat-screen TV. We didn't have one until Grandpa came to live here. Mom calls it "the price of built-in babysitting."

Grandpa searches down the back of his chair. He pats down his pockets, too. "Heh, heh," he laughs. "That little devil remote's got legs, Mikey Boy. I swear it. Always running away from me."

"Got it, Grandpa." I spot it on the windowsill right away.

"Good recon, son," he says.

As I hand it over I whisper, "Am I in trouble, Grandpa?"

He turns the volume up rather than down so Mom won't hear and winks. "Not that I know of, Mikey. Want me in there?"

I wrinkle my nose. "Nah," I say. "As long as she's not on the war path."

Grandpa shakes his head. "Want to watch a war movie

later?" Grandpa loves war movies. I feel guilty about my report for a second, then I put my thumbs up. Only then does Grandpa turn the volume down. "Never can get it right," he says loudly with another wink.

"Mikey?" Mom beckons from the kitchen. "Quick. I've got to leave in five minutes." She pats the chair next to her. We're on the same level so I know she's serious. I try to look interested in an innocent sort of way, but I'm clenching my teeth, waiting for a lecture.

"Mikey," she says, "I don't want to worry you, but I've just got an email from school. All the parents have. Apparently a fourth grader was…frightened…by a man who jumped out at him this morning. Nothing bad happened. The man didn't rob the boy or hurt him, but it was just on Swinton Street, close to the park on Alvarado. The kid was on his way to school. Have you heard anything? Do you know who the kid was?"

I wait before I speak, thinking through what she's said. She's not mad. She doesn't know we were there. It's OK. "Yeah," I say. "Yeah, it was Ryan O'Driscoll. He was late to school. They sent him to see Miss Wendy. A lady in the laundromat found him or something."

Mom shakes her head. "As if that family hasn't got enough going on." She's sort of talking to herself. "I'd better email his mom." She walks over to the living room door and leans in. "Dad? Would you mind walking

Mikey and Kyler to school for the next few days? Just to be on the safe side?"

"Sure," Grandpa says.

"And maybe one other kid, if he needs it?" she asks.

"Fine by me. As long as the kid doesn't run off, because I'm not chasing after anyone anymore." He taps his right leg beneath the knee, as if Mom hasn't noticed the false one for the last forty years. "I can't even keep the remote in order. That right, Mikey?"

I don't answer because I'm thinking. If we have Grandpa with us, we can't look for our Celt. This is going to ruin everything. And then I think, "extra kid?" We're going to have an extra kid tagging along, too?

Mom taps out an email and says, "There. I don't expect anything will come of it, but at least I've tried. Mikey, Grandpa's going to walk you and Kyler to school for the next few days until all this has blown over. You won't mind walking with Ryan too, will you?"

"Ryan?" I say. "*Ryan?*" But it's too late. Mom's already out the door.

CHAPTER TEN

"Do we have to pick up Ryan, Grandpa?" I ask at breakfast. "Can't you walk him to school and I'll walk with Kyler?"

"No, Mikey Boy. Your mom sent this list while she was working her shift, and it's numbered. No stars or abc's. Numbers. You know what that means. Orders are orders." He points to a printed email on the table:

1) Get up and leave house 15 minutes early.
2) Give M carrot and jicama sticks in fridge for snack.
3) Make sure M takes his coat.
4) Pick up Kyler.
5) Pick up Ryan O'Driscoll, 1110 Alvarado. He'll be waiting on the street at 7:45.
6) Mikey, walk with Grandpa. Don't run ahead. Tell Kyler too.

"Oh, man. Ryan hates us. This stinks," I say.

"Hates you?" Grandpa hands me a bag of chips and three gummy worms from his poker store.

"It's not just me, Grandpa. He's mean to everyone right now."

"Hmmm," Grandpa says. "Well, he won't be mean when I'm around. Besides, Mikey, you have to remember, I've met some real mean guys in my time, but most of them had someone do mean things to them first. Be nice to people, Mikey, because everyone's fighting a hard battle." He forms his hand into a fist and pretends to bonk me over the head with it.

When we ring Kyler's doorbell, Kyler's mom answers the door while yelling back down the hallway, "Hurry up! And take your coat. It's cold."

"Awww, Mom. Nooo," Kyler whines from the kitchen.

"It's cold, Kyler! Isn't it cold, Mikey? Mikey says it's cold." I swear I haven't said a thing. "Take your coat!" Mariko's dressed in her emergency room gear. She looks tired, but she still smiles at Grandpa and says, "Thank you so much for doing this, Marty. Are your wrist and leg OK?"

Grandpa twirls his wrist around in front of her then pulls up his pants' leg. His three stitches are neat as anything, and his cut is closed up and pink.

"Wow, Marty. That looks good," she says. "You heal real fast…for an old guy." She gives him a playful pat on the shoulder.

"Old soldier!" Grandpa corrects her. "Heh, heh, heh." Mariko laughs along with him. She's the only one who can call Grandpa an old guy and get away with it. "Good genes and good luck! That's what gets me through every time," Grandpa says.

Losing a leg doesn't seem like good luck to me, but Grandpa always tells me, "I was one of the lucky ones. I came home."

Kyler pushes past his mom to join us.

"OK," Mariko says. "Have a good day, and don't run ahead!"

We walk far enough in front of Grandpa to talk, but not so far that it looks like we're running off. He's happy walking behind us at his own pace, saying good morning to the people he knows, and saluting them with his stick; people like the white-haired English lady with the yappy dog and the grocery store guy.

"What's Ryan gonna say when we pick him up?" Kyler whispers. "Will he tell on us to your Grandpa?

"I hope not." The thought makes me uneasy inside. "Grandpa'd have to tell Mom and she'd be M-A-D, mad."

"Mine too." Kyler hitches up his backpack. "And how are we going to find our warrior again if we're always with people?"

"I've been thinking about that. Like you said, the Celt found us, didn't he, even when we were with Ryan? He could be watching us right now." As I speak, I feel it—that sensation of someone staring at the back of my head. I spin around and Grandpa grins at me. Well, duh!

"Yeah, I guess." Kyler sighs. "But if Ryan calls me Turtle again, I'll cream him." Kyler's as disappointed as I am about this whole "walking Ryan to school" thing, so I whisper, "Look, we get to walk straight past the alley every day we walk Ryan to school. That's perfect. We couldn't have arranged it better ourselves. We can't get to Park Two when we're walking with Ryan and Grandpa, that's tough, but we never got to search in Big…uh… Lost Tooth…er, I mean Park One, did we? So it's great we're going there again. Maybe we can persuade Grandpa to let us scout it out while we wait for Ryan. We can pretend we're covert operations: a crack team of two, handpicked for our mega-awesome fighting skills. Urban ninja, Kyler!" I don't mention "turtles" in the same sentence as "ninja" for obvious reasons.

Kyler's face brightens. He glances around and throws himself against the wall of a town house, as if he's a shadow not a person. "Garage water heater, strapped all around with duct tape, tucked into the duct tape bands!"

"Clever," I say. Kyler grins and then slinks the whole way to Alvarado.

Just our luck, Ryan is already waiting outside a bright-yellow house when we arrive. That leaves us no time to check out the park. His house must be newly painted because there's still a painter's sign in the yard. There are Mexican tiles up to the front door and twisty bushes cut into pompoms along the front, like Dr. Seuss trees. It's pretty much opposite the park, so it's no wonder he goes running there.

Grandpa introduces himself, even though Ryan's seen him loads of times at school and knows who he is. Ryan glares at us. "I don't need you to walk me to school. It was that dumb lady at the laundromat who wouldn't leave me alone. I wasn't frightened. My dad's a Sergeant."

"Oh, I know that, son," Grandpa says quietly, "but this isn't about you being afraid. It's about your mom and the other moms being afraid. They just want you to be safe. No point taking risks unless you need to."

"If nothing happens, I can walk on my own again, right?"

"Right," Grandpa says. "In a few days."

Ryan glances across the street, chewing the inside of his mouth. Then he hurries in front of us, so no one will think he's with us. Grandpa calls for him to slow down. Ryan turns and scowls, but he waits.

"Sergeant, eh?" Grandpa asks when he catches up. "Me too."

Kyler nods toward the park and gives me a resigned look. I nod back. He's right. There's no time to search the park. This morning is a disaster so far.

I wait a minute watching them all walk ahead of me. For someone who says he's not afraid, Ryan's looking around an awful lot. I guess he's looking for the Celt, too, wondering if he'll surprise us again.

I scan the street one more time and check out the park entrance. No Celt. As I look away, I catch the number of Ryan's house. It says 1113. I look again. I'm sure Mom wrote 1110 in her email.

On the opposite side of the street, next to the park, there's a house with a rusty metal screen over the front door. The house is painted a yucky green. Damp clumps of plaster are peeling off the walls revealing patches of old brown paint and black mold. Inside the front window, yellowing stacks of mail pile up against the glass. The curtains of the house move slightly. There's a dark shadow behind them that gradually disappears. I look at the number by the door. A zero hangs to one side, almost falling off. 1110 it says.

CHAPTER ELEVEN

"Hey, wait for me," I yell. The others are already walking past the alley where the Celt jumped us. I get this tingling feeling, the same as when you bite a piece of foil by mistake. Will the Celt be there?

I decide to tell Kyler about Ryan's house later, just in case he makes a big deal of it. There's something weird about pretending to live in someone else's house, and I don't want Kyler to call it and make Ryan mad again.

When I catch up, Kyler's pointing down the alley saying, "He jumped out from here!"

Shoot! He's not supposed to know that. We weren't supposed to be on this street when it happened. I glare at him, and he goes red.

Luckily, Grandpa doesn't seem to notice. He just says, "That right, Ryan?" I'm sure Ryan's going to spill the beans. He glances at me, and then nods in answer. "Like an ambush?" Grandpa asks. Ryan nods again. "Very scary."

Grandpa puts his hand on Ryan's shoulder and steers him down the street. Kyler and I look at each other, eyes wide. Ryan didn't get us into trouble. Why? He could have so easily.

An Asian lady comes to the door of the laundromat as we pass. She crosses her arms. "That boy needs to stay away from him," she says.

Grandpa nods his head in agreement. "That's right. Thank you. Good morning," he says.

She wishes him good morning too and smiles.

"It was her," Ryan says. "She walked me to school. I didn't need her to."

"I'm sure you didn't, Ryan," Grandpa says, "but she was just trying to help." Grandpa's voice gets lower. "Did I tell you I got ambushed once? Scariest day of my army career." Kyler and I stay close, so we can overhear what they're saying. "Everything was completely out of control. Couldn't keep my men together, didn't know where the enemy were coming from, nothing. One of my friends took a bullet in the shoulder right next to me…and when I was trying to get him up, another bullet went straight under my arm into his chest and killed him. I feel sweat breaking out just thinking about it. Sometimes things are out of our control, Ryan, and it's not our fault."

Kyler gives me a "that's strange" look. I do the same back. Ryan walks next to Grandpa all the way to school.

At the door to our classroom, Grandpa pats Ryan on the back. "Don't forget to show those teachers how smart you are, just in case they haven't noticed yet. Heh, heh." It's what he always says to Kyler and me.

As Grandpa heads home across the blacktop and Kyler struggles through the door with his backpack, Ryan steps in front of me and mumbles, "You forget about that guy and I won't tell on you, OK?"

I say OK before I can even process what Ryan means. I'm cool with keeping quiet, but only because I don't want people to find out about our Celt. But everyone in the school already knows that Ryan was practically mugged by someone. As Grandpa says, that ship has already sailed. Ryan can't hide it now.

At recess, I tell Kyler about Ryan's house. "Why pretend to live in a different house?" I ask. "I mean, it's kind of dumb."

"If I lived in a dump," Kyler says, "I'd pretend to live somewhere else, too."

"But why is his house such a dump?"

Kyler shrugs. "Dunno. Maybe his mom doesn't like doing house stuff much. Maybe she's sick. Could be a lot of reasons."

"OK, but why does he want us to forget about the Celt? I mean we're not telling anyone about him anyway."

"Yeah, but Ryan doesn't know that." Kyler grins. "He's worried we'll tell everyone how afraid he was. It'll ruin his rep. Of course he wants us to keep quiet." All the way back to class he imitates Ryan. "No," he squeaks. "Just go!"

>> >> >>

That evening, after I scrape out a couple of paragraphs for that report I never finished, Grandpa and I watch some of *The Longest Day*. It's a World War II movie about the D-Day landings when the Allies invaded France to free Europe from the Nazis. It's Grandpa's favorite. I've seen it before, but I'm fine with seeing it again. I'm trying to see as many movies as I can while I have the chance. When Dad comes home and Grandpa moves back to his house, I'm guessing he'll take the giant TV with him. He likes the big screen.

Of course, Grandpa might not move back to his house at all. I overheard Mom and Mariko talking one time. Mom said she'd asked Grandpa to come and help while Dad's away because it was the perfect excuse to get him to move in. "Dad thinks he's helping me," she said, "but really I can keep an eye on him. I love his old house, but it's way too much work for him now. If he gets used to living here, we could turn the garage into an apartment for him." I think that would be really cool, and we'd get to keep the TV.

Anyway, Grandpa and I are eating chocolate-covered

peppermints, and we've just got to the part where the teenage soldier gets shot because he mistakes the sound of a gun bolt for the secret D-Day signal, when we hear the front door open.

"Hi, Dad! Mikey!" Mom's home early. She never comes home before the end of her shift. Never.

I jump up. "Quick," I whisper to Grandpa, "switch it off."

"The dang thing," Grandpa says, twisting in his chair. He's lost the remote again.

"I have a terrible headache, and I'm aching all over," Mom calls from the kitchen. "I just have to get to bed. Some kind of bug, I guess." I dash for the TV. Too late! She's in the doorway just as the screen goes black.

"Oh, Dad. Not war movies again. I specifically said no war movies."

"But it's a good—"

"We agreed!"

"It's an old one, not *Jarhead* or *Hurt*—"

"Not on a school night, Dad. Has Mikey even finished his book report yet? Besides I don't want him seeing all that stuff, glorifying war and violence. Everyone seems to think it's OK for kids to go around pretending to shoot people, but I'm sorry, I don't."

"OK, OK!" Grandpa waves his hand at me. I scramble to put the DVD back in its box. "But this was my life, remember!" he says.

"Yeah and mine too, but I didn't choose it, you did, and it wasn't so great for a while. Remember that?" Mom turns her head away. Grandpa catches sight of the remote under his newspaper and points it toward the TV, even though it's already off. We stand in silence for a few awkward moments.

When Mom says, "Just go to bed, Mikey," I'm so out of there. She reaches in her pocket for a tissue as I slip past her. "I'm sorry, honey, I've got a cold or something is all." She blows her nose. I hurry upstairs.

As I reach my bedroom door, I hear Mom mention Ryan. Grandpa always tells me there's never any good in an overheard conversation, but I creep back to the top of the stairs to listen.

"Was Ryan all right this morning, Dad?" Mom and Grandpa move into the kitchen. Mom rattles through the plastic medicine box in the top cupboard. "You didn't say how it went. I should have asked when I got up this afternoon, but I forgot." She's trying to change the subject.

"Everything was fine. Just a normal walk to school. Didn't see anyone," Grandpa says. "Ryan didn't want to come at first." His voice drops. Mom says something like, "I think he's still there," and I have to tiptoe down a few steps to keep on listening. "Sylvia seems to be having a really hard time. I used to chat with her a little before pick-up, but I haven't seen her in months. She just sort of clammed up and then disappeared. One of the other moms told me she's struggling with depression or something. Very sad. I wish I knew them better, but I never see her, and Mikey doesn't play with Ryan anymore."

Grandpa grunts. "It's hard on a family," he says, gruffly.

"It is," Mom says, "and yet you still show him war movies and wonder why I get mad? Especially after all those years—"

"I'll see Mikey to bed," Grandpa says.

Later that night, I hear Mom talking on the phone. She's walking around her bedroom, and she's crying. Panic rises in my chest, like bubbles racing to the top of a soda. I sure hope Dad's OK.

My dad's not a soldier or anything. He's an engineer, but he works in some dangerous countries. He's in Nigeria right now, and engineers have been kidnapped there. Mom tries not to talk about it too much, but I heard her telling Mariko that she didn't want him to take another job like this. She said she's had enough of being nervous and scared all the time, and it wasn't worth the risk, even if he does get paid a lot. She was really angry with him for going this time.

When Mom's voice gets louder, I slip out of bed and creep onto the landing. There's no light beneath the bedroom door. Mom's walking around in the dark.

I listen, wondering what's happened. If there's something wrong why doesn't she wake Grandpa? Then I realize it's Grandpa she's talking about, and it's Dad she's talking to.

"This is my house, and Mikey's my son," she's saying. "I should be able to bring him up the way I want. Dad should respect that, Jeff." There's a pause. "No, I'm not denying his experience, but has it ever occurred to you that he's denying mine? All you guys stick together, but you're wrong. War's wrong. You being away is wrong!" and she starts crying again. There's a long pause. "I'm sorry," she sobs, "I feel awful, and I miss you…"

I go back to bed. It's just like Mom to get all worked up over nothing. Sounds like Dad is just fine. I miss him, too, but we videochat on the weekends.

As I get back into bed, I wonder what Ryan thinks when his mom is on the phone at night. His dad *is* at war.

CHAPTER TWELVE

"This is torture." Kyler and I are eating lunch at the tables outside and finally finishing our epic battle in *Romanii: Northern Borders*. We never get to bring tablets to school normally, but we needed them for a video project for art class so our moms let us, just this once. We even got special permission from Miss O'Brien, so we kind of feel we have permission to play games during lunch, too. We make sure we hide at the end of a table, hunched over, so the other kids won't see.

"Torture?" Kyler makes a face. "You've just defeated every Roman legion I've got. You've pushed back the Roman invasion, just like you've always dreamed. Marcus Julius—me—is a mere shell of his former self. I'm going back to the Roman senate in disgrace, Mikey, and you say you're tortured? I lost. I let down the entire Roman Empire! Think about it." Kyler's holding his head in his hands, hunched over his screen. I should be loving this victory, but all I can think of is the Celt.

I flip the tablet cover over the screen. "We didn't see him today. We didn't see him yesterday. If the laundromat is the gateway to the Otherworld, why wasn't he there the last two days like he was on Tuesday? Believe me, I don't want him jumping out on us again—"

"You've just won, Mikey!"

"I know, but where is he? It's torture!"

Kyler shrugs, which makes me crazy because he does not seem anywhere near as upset as I am. Then he says, quietly, "I think we've already lost him. He disappeared on Tuesday, in the alley. He's already back in his own—"

"Stop!" I can't even let him finish. I can't believe this is my "Dr. Time Travel" sidekick talking, letting our incredible adventure swirl down the drain. I look at the ground. There's a stain on the blacktop. We're sitting right where I told Kyler about the Celt on Monday, where he spilled his chocolate milk. It's only been four days, and he's giving up already, before the chocolate milk stain has even washed away.

I'm so mad I lean right over the lunch table, grab one of Kyler's cheese sticks and point it back at him. "You saw him! You can't deny it! And it was you who put the 'Celts in the Otherworld' theory together—"

"That was your idea, dude, you were awesome—"

"And now you're saying you can't even be bothered to look for him anymore?"

I fix him with my Celtic-pride stare, the one I've been practicing in the mirror. I imagine I'm a Celt, just like our warrior, with blue tattoos and a golden torc around my neck. I'm just about to beat the best Romans in the whole imperial army. I hold Kyler with my eyes, until he looks all shifty and ashamed. "We agreed he may be going backward and forward from the Otherworld to here, or he may still be here, waiting for Halloween. We agreed on that, Kyler."

"Yeah, but—" He looks even more uncomfortable, which is only right.

I wave the cheese stick. "So if he's waiting for Halloween then he's still here somewhere, in the alley or one of the parks. If he's going backward and forward in the Otherworld wormhole, well, it doesn't move around, does it? It's right here by the laundromat, so the reason we can't find him is that…" Kyler tries to grab his cheese stick back, but I pull it away. With my other hand, I pick up one of Mom's jicama sticks, crunch down and, eureka! The crunch factor works again. "Either he's hiding too darn well…or the conditions are wrong!"

"How do you figure that?" Kyler says. He lets his mouth hang open, which is gross because there's still sushi in there, but at least it shows he's thinking, so I let it pass.

"Because…" I pause, swinging my arm like I'm winding up for a pitch, "when we saw him on Tuesday, it was really foggy, remember? The last two days we haven't had any fog. That's the problem. The Celts were all about fog."

"That's it, Mikey." Kyler makes a fist and shakes it at the sickeningly sunny sky. "It's October for goodness' sake. What's with the sun, world?"

I throw Kyler his cheese stick and slam the table with my palm. I have Kyler onboard again and it feels great. "So, either we wait for a foggy day or we need to be looking for him at night or really early morning, when there's definitely fog."

"At dusk and dawn!" Kyler chokes on his California roll. "Oh yeah!" he wheezes.

"It's so simple I can't believe we didn't think of it before." I look to Kyler, expecting his eyes to be popping with excitement, but they're wide and watering instead. I guess he's still choking. I slap him on the back, and he stamps his feet on the ground until he gets his voice back.

"Swallowed the wrong way," he rasps, "but yes, yes, and yes! Operation Getaceltorix, Part Two." He does his low, movie-trailer voice. It sounds even huskier than normal because of the choking. "The Night Hunt."

I join in. "They said it could not be, but two boys know the truth, and they won't stop until they've proved it!"

We stuff the tablets and the rest of our lunch in our backpacks and act out the whole thing in the yard. Why eat when you can pretend to find a Celt at night?

"So we're ninjas creeping down Swinton," Kyler

says as we sidle down the edge of the blacktop toward the foursquare courts, where Ryan is arguing whether he's out or not. "And the door to the laundromat is glowing with orange light."

Then it's my turn. "Pretend I can see the laundromat lady, and her eyes are so red it's like they're on fire."

"Then the warrior leaps out, his sword gleaming in the street lights!" Kyler yells.

"I spin to the left before the sword falls and run down the alley—"

"And I'm left facing him." Kyler looks up as if he's seeing the Celt in front of him. Not moving his eyes from the Celt's intense stare, he beckons for me to join him.

"So I run up the wall, do a backflip, and land right between you and him," I whisper. "And he's just about to slice the sword right through my head when I pull out some…" I hesitate a moment, "some beef jerky—"

"Beef jerky?" Kyler says.

"Yeah, and I hand it to him, and the sword stops an inch from my head because he's never seen beef jerky before, and it smells better than any food he's tasted."

"That's lame," Kyler says. "You're gonna save me with beef jerky?"

"He's a Celtic berserker, Kyler, and there's nothing those guys like better than meat. Beef jerky would be amazing to him. We have to convince him we're friends, so we give him a present."

"But beef jerky?"

"Well, we can't buy him a beer. Anyway, beef jerky makes perfect sense. It's like roasted boar."

"Why not give him some of my mom's sushi?"

It takes me a second to realize Kyler's kidding. He's not into the gift idea at all. Our game goes on hold as we argue whether distracting the Celt with beef jerky is better than a Tae Kwon Do kick to his chest. I'm demonstrating how hard it would be to even reach his chest, when I notice Ryan eyeing us from the foursquare court. I wonder how much he's heard, because he's really staring. It spooks me.

I grab Kyler's arm and say, "Let's talk about this later."

Kyler's smug. "Know you're losing, Mikey?"

"Yeah. You win," I say to shut him up.

Kyler knows I never give up that easily. "What's up?" he mouths.

"Tell you later." I drag him to the other side of the blacktop.

"What is it?"

"Don't look now, but Ryan was listening."

"So what?" Kyler says, looking around. "It was a dumb game anyway, once you brought in the beef jerky."

"But he looked strange," I say. "He was mad at us for playing the game. I kind of told him we'd forget about the whole laundromat incident."

"Chill, Mikey. We didn't even mention him in the game." The bell rings for end of recess. "And he always looks strange." As Kyler sprints ahead of me to class he yells, "Toilet flush tank! Plastic box at the bottom!"

"Yuck," I say.

"Oh, and kick to the chest. No contest!"

》 》 》

On the way back home Kyler asks, "Are you serious about doing this?"

"What?"

"Going out at night."

"Of course," I say. "How else are we going to find him? We just have to pick a night when both our moms are on the night shift. Grandpa will never hear me leave the house. We'll take flashlights, and we'll only stay out for, say, fifteen minutes. Just enough time to walk to the alley, see if he's there, and come back again."

Kyler looks worried. "We can take cell phones, too."

"Sure," I say. "Unless you're chicken." I can't believe I've used the "chicken dare." I'm just as nervous as Kyler is, but once I've said it, there's no turning back.

"I'm not chicken. Unless you are."

"I'm not," I have to say.

"Then we should go tonight. Mom's working."

"But my mom's home. We have to find a night when they're both out," I say. "We'll text."

"Dad-sized rain boot, old sock, stuffed in the toe," Kyler says. "And I'm most definitely in!"

CHAPTER THIRTEEN

I'm eating dinner with Grandpa later that night when Mom comes down the stairs in her uniform.

"No war movies tonight, Dad," she says.

"Don't worry, there's a game on. I'm not missing that for the Second World War, Vietnam, or Desert Storm!" Grandpa chuckles.

"Mikey should be in bed by half past eight. Make sure he finishes that book report." I groan inwardly, though I keep staring at my plate pretending I'm not listening. I hate reports!

"Oh…and Ryan doesn't need walking to school tomorrow. His mom emailed and said she's fine with him going alone again. Anything else? Oh…be good, Mikey."

I look up from my macaroni and cheese. "But it's not your work night tonight." Mom gestures that I should wipe my mouth. I don't even complain because I can't believe my luck. I should have guessed when she didn't come down to eat.

"I know, honey. I'm sorry. I'd love to stay home, but I have to make up that shift I missed. I feel so much better today." She gives me a peck on the cheek and tells

Grandpa to enjoy the game. I try to look disappointed, but right now I could do a cartwheel.

"Want to watch the game with me, Mikey Boy?" Grandpa asks as Mom leaves. "Boys' night in?"

I'm too busy texting Kyler under the table to answer for a moment. "What? Oh, no thanks, Grandpa. I have that report and then my model of Rome to finish."

"Oh yeah, your report. Better get that done. Here," Grandpa hands me some gummy worms, "C-rations for your special mission."

"Thanks, Grandpa."

The minute I'm upstairs, Kyler and I text at top speed. We agree to meet at four thirty in the morning because, according to the Internet, that's when the fog is due to come in.

I go to bed with my PJs over my jeans and sweat-shirt. I'm so puffed up I look like a football mascot. My jeans ride up inside my PJ legs, and I can't swing my arms, but I've seen kids do this in movies, and it always works for them.

When Grandpa looks in on his way to bed, I'll be in my PJs, so he'll think everything's normal. When four twenty comes, I'll throw them off quick, and my real clothes will be underneath. Next, I'll stuff pillows end to end down the bed and curve them around so it looks like I'm asleep under the covers. That's just in case Grandpa looks in on me. I know he won't because he has to get his leg on at night, but I want to be sure. Then, I'll creep down the stairs and out the door. Like I said, they do it in movies all the time.

I'd like to stay up all night until we're ready to leave, but I'm not sure I can, so I set my cell phone alarm for four twenty and shove it under my pillow. In the First World War, they say that soldiers propped their eyes open with matchsticks so they wouldn't fall asleep on night duty. They'd be shot if they did. I wonder if I should try it, but the idea of poking my eyes out by mistake is too gross. Guess you only try stuff like that if you risk being shot.

I switch off my light and look at the glow-stars Mom put on my bedroom wall when I was tiny. They're supposed to be in the shape of constellations, but so many have dropped off that I've stopped putting them back in the right place. Instead, I reconfigure them into battles. Each star is a soldier, and the large ones are cavalry or tanks. Sometimes, I imagine they're Napoleon invading Russia, sometimes the D-Day landings.

Tonight, it's Romans versus Celts. I'm a Celt, of course, and I'm trying to outflank the Romans with my fastest charioteers. Not that the Celts were really into strategy, except for one thing. Much as they loved war, they avoided full-out battles if they could. They'd try to frighten their opponents away first, with their whole "scary hair, tattoos, chanting, and eerie-sounding horns" deal. If that didn't work, they had champions battle it out one-on-one, so only two people got hurt, not the whole tribe. Full-out battles were only a last resort. The Romans never understood that. They were all about full-blown extermination.

I wake to the sound of my alarm through the pillow. I knew I'd fall asleep. I slip out of bed and pull off my PJs, but my brain isn't in gear yet. I end up wrestling with my PJ top over my head, groping for the flashlight, and nearly knocking it to the floor, and then stumbling on the shoes I left by the door.

Kyler texts.

> Meet me in street
> 5 mins

I reply.

> Cooooooool

Though I'm seventy miles from cool right now.

I take a deep breath to calm myself, open my door really slowly, and wait on the landing until I hear Grandpa snore. He reminds me of a purring cat. Then I tiptoe down the stairs and pull on my shoes. That part turns out to be so easy I feel almost cheated. I could do this every night and no one would notice.

It's colder than I was expecting. The street glows a creepy, blurry yellow under the streetlamps. It's definitely foggy, just as we'd hoped. I peer through the mist down the sidewalk toward Kyler's house. He said he'd be waiting for me, but he's not there. I hope he hasn't gotten caught. No, he's probably hiding, ready to jump out and scare me half to death. That's the sort of thing he finds funny. I scan the lines of parked cars.

Everything's quiet and soft at the edges. It's spooky. There are no cars driving by, no one coming out of their houses, nothing. It takes me a few seconds to realize I can hear a TV even at this hour, and the streetlights are buzzing, and there's a police siren wailing a few blocks away.

The VA stands at the top of our street on a hill. It's a tall building with lights on at every level, making halos in the mist. It makes me think of a rocket ready for takeoff. I can almost believe it could blast into space, but I bet the people inside aren't getting much sleep with all those lights shining. Grandpa says the VA is great, as far as he's concerned, but a hospital is still the worst place to be sick.

I tell him that doesn't make sense, but Grandpa always says, "I tried it once, and the nurses woke me every four hours to check my pulse and temperature. 'Listen,' I said, 'if I'm dead can't you just wait until morning to find out, because if I'm alive I'd rather have my sleep.'" When Grandpa tells Mariko this story he always winks, and she tells him he's a funny man. He likes that.

An ambulance pulls slowly into the sweeping driveway of the hospital, its lights flashing red. I like seeing the ambulance people still at work. Knowing that there are doctors, taxi drivers, people like Mom, working all over the city, even in the middle of the night, makes me feel better. And, right now, Dad is already at work because it's morning in Nigeria. Weird.

I start down the sidewalk toward Kyler's house. The streetlights cast circles of yellow onto the ground like giant stepping stones. I tell myself the dark spots are black holes to parallel universes where monster lice rule the world and suck your face off, so, obviously, I don't want to step there. I jump from light to light, but I'm bored of it by the time I get to Kyler's. Guess he'd have jumped me by now if he was going to.

I start to get mad. He texted me to make sure I was awake. Five minutes, he said. I stand at the bottom of the steps to his house, underneath a big potted lemon tree, glaring at his front door.

Two seconds later, the trash can at the corner of Kyler's tiny front yard crashes to the ground. I cry out like a cat that's had its tail squished and jump behind the lemon tree, grazing my hand on a thorn.

A raccoon, the size of a dog, flashes her bandit mask at me through the mist. She chases the trash can through three revolutions before batting it to a stop and thrusting her head inside. Two babies scamper behind her.

The noise of the raccoon ripping trash is enough to wake people ten miles away, so I'm not surprised when Kyler's front door flies open. I'm sure I'm busted, but it's Kyler slinking out, not his dad. Kyler meets my gaze then flattens himself against the wall just as a window upstairs grinds open.

Kyler does a goofy "oops, I messed up" grin. I reply with my "sure did and where've you been anyway" glare.

Kyler's dad leans out of the bedroom window. He's wearing a baggy sweatshirt, and his hair sticks up around his head like a fuzz ball. "Darn raccoons," he slurs in a sleepy voice. "Scat."

The mama raccoon pulls her head out of the can. She has a butter wrapper stuck to one ear, which she wipes off on the ground. The babies try to lick it. Dave sighs. "You're not afraid, are you?" he says to the raccoon. The raccoon shakes her head. I guess she's got butter in her ear, but it looks like she's saying "no." Dave pulls the window back down.

"Quick!" Kyler jumps down the steps, grabs my arm and pulls us behind a parked car in the street.

A few seconds later, Dave opens the front door. "Go

on, scat!" He stomps down the steps, muttering angrily, "I keep telling her to use the special elastic. It's already attached to the can lid, for Pete's sake." A light switches on in the neighbor's house.

The mama raccoon scampers up the street dragging a white garbage bag behind her. The babies follow. When the bag splits, wrappers, milk cartons, and a greasy pizza box spill into the gutter. The babies jump over themselves in surprise. I can't help it. I snort through my nose loud as a pig. Kyler throws his hand over my face and we duck down so low I can smell the oil stains on the asphalt.

Dave stops to listen. I hold my breath, as if that'll help me stay still. I'm pretty sure Kyler's holding his breath too, because his cheeks are all puffed up. It must work because after a few seconds, Dave says, "Like it's too much effort to put the lid on right."

We hear the trash can scrape along the ground and the wheels rattle, as Dave trundles the can back into place. He stomps back up the steps and slams the door.

"Man, your dad is grumpy tonight," I say.

"His team lost," Kyler whispers. Then his mouth hangs open in thinking mode. He shakes my arm. "Oh, no. What are we gonna do? He'll look in my bedroom to check on me."

"Did you do the 'pillows down the bed' thing?"

Kyler looks blank. We don't have time to think. I push

him into the open. "Pretend like you're trying to get back in. Quick!" I say and dodge behind the car again.

Kyler runs up the steps as his dad flings open the front door. "Kyler! Thank God! There you are!"

"Phew, Dad!" he says. "I was just about to freak. I was trying to get back in. You locked me out, and it's freezing out here in this fog." He sounds a bit fake, like a kid in a sitcom, but it seems to work.

"Trying to get back in?" Kyler's dad was not expecting that. "You were? But what are you doing outside?"

"Boy, Dad, didn't you hear the noise? There were a whole bunch of raccoons around the trash cans. I chased them down the street."

"You got changed?"

"No!" Kyler pulls his PJ top out from underneath his sweatshirt. "Just threw some clothes over my PJs."

"Kyler, it could have been robbers or anything."

"I could see it was raccoons, Dad. Whole family. The mom must have doubled back on me. She was huge."

Dave puts his arm around Kyler's shoulder. "Don't go doing that again. I'm the raccoon chaser around here, OK?" As Dave leads him into the house, Kyler looks back at me and sticks out his lower lip. I know what he's trying to say: our adventure is over. Darn raccoons.

I sit down on the sidewalk. Being out at night with a friend is an adventure. On your own it's more scary. It's not that I'm a coward, but I'm not stupid either. Who knows what could happen out here in the dark? I should go home.

I let my chin drop onto my chest. I really don't want to give in when I've only just started. I'm looking for the Celt after all. This is the biggest and best adventure I've ever had. The only adventure I've ever had. I can't walk away now. I imagine I'm a soldier at the end of a battle. I'm a Celt, wounded after a raid on the Romans, but I have to rescue my best friend who's been taken captive in a nearby fort. I return my sword to its scabbard, heave myself up on my spear, glance down the battlefield—and I see my Celt materialize out of the mist.

He's running up the road toward me.

My heart does a drum solo, a hundred beats a minute.

CHAPTER FOURTEEN

I dodge back down behind the car. It's awesome. I've found him, but now that I've found him I don't know what to do. The way he's running scares me. He's intense. Is he running to find the portal to the Otherworld before it closes? Is he mad because he's come back to this time that he doesn't want to be in?

I peer from my hiding place. There's no one behind him, so he's not running away from anyone. Next minute, there's a crash further up the street as the raccoon knocks over another trash can. The Celt throws himself down and covers his ears. "No, no, no," he mutters. He stays there for a long time. Then he's crouching, swigging from a bottle, standing, and sprinting up the street again. His arms are pumping. He's concentrating so hard he doesn't even look at me.

As he races past, he mutters in his strange accent, "He took his great barbed spear and thrust it into the air." I smell beer—the same smell that's in the kitchen on poker nights—but I don't care. In the excitement, my fear melts away and I race after him. My arms are tingling. My chest feels electric. The hairs on the back of my neck prickle like a dog's. I'm terrified and completely alive at the same time. I run as fast as I can to keep up.

"He took the shield and raised it, but the dragon flew out of the sun. Even shielding his eyes, the warrior couldn't see for the rays of light. But as the dragon's talons stretched to grasp him, the spear hit its target. The dragon exploded in a mighty roar. It burst the warrior's eardrums and forced the blood swirling from them like water out of a shell plucked from the sea."

Whoa! This is something else. The Celt sounds like he's reciting poetry.

"And the dragon spewed forth fire, which flowed like molten lava. Gobbets of flame licked the heavens above and colored the sky black. The warrior leaped through the flame as a salmon leaps up river. He grasped the scaly sides of the beast and plunged his sword again and again into the burning heart of the creature. The beast screamed, twisting and turning in its agony…"

The Celt hesitates as he reaches the cross street at the top of our road, right by my house. I dodge behind a trash can, not wanting to distract him from whatever it is he's doing.

"And the warrior ripped open the belly of the dragon and pulled forth, from the body of the beast, the three men it had swallowed. Three good men, half eaten but still alive, and he cursed the beast that it ever lived!"

I wish Kyler was here because I can't work out what's happening. It doesn't fit any of our theories. The Celt is living some battle that I can't see. It's either in his head, or it's actually happening to him right now, which means his body might be in our time, but the things he's experiencing are in another dimension. Maybe he's only half traveled from the Otherworld. Maybe it's some parallel universe or different dimension thing that Kyler would totally get, but I don't. All I know is, it's so realistic that I can breathe it, sense it, feel it with him.

When he says he's wielding his sword, somehow I can see it. His arm tenses and sways with the weight of the weapon. When he slices through the air, I swear I hear the sword swish. When he pulls at the bodies of the men, getting them under their shoulders, dragging them across the sidewalk, his spine bends over with the weight. His eyes are shiny, and the muscles in his neck are as tight as fishing line.

As the Celt pulls the third invisible body onto the sidewalk, he jerks his head up. "He hears another man in the stomach of the dragon calling for help," he mutters. I swallow. My throat tightens. "The warrior maiden has never made it easy, and she's not going to now." The Celt straightens up, places his legs apart, glares at a streetlight overhead and carries on talking. "How strong are you, warrior?' she taunts. Her voice echoes like thunder through the clouds of black smoke. Her eyes flash like fireballs. 'How much can you take?'"

He stays there for a moment, as if hypnotized, his hands opening and closing at his sides, and then he strides toward the road. He's not looking left or right or anywhere except at whatever action is playing out in front of him. At the last second, he stops at the curb. He puts his arm out to the side as if he's holding people back. "Don't!" he says. "Wait!"

There's nothing but the insect buzz of the streetlights above us. He scans the road. I guess he's looking for traffic, but the longer he waits the more I get to thinking he's looking for something else. He kneels down and stares across the road from a different angle. "We got another one. Soda can! In the gutter," he cries as he spins around, looking up at the rooftops. It's like he's looking for someone to blame for the trash, but it was the raccoon. Anyone can see that.

"Another damned soda can!" he says and swears a whole bunch more.

I don't understand why he's so worried about a soda can. They didn't even have them in his time. But something has changed because the Celt is alert now in a way he wasn't before. His eyes seem so round that he's like an owl, twisting his head slowly, looking at everything on the street. A chip bag rustles in the gutter, and the Celt is right there watching it. The streetlight flickers and he turns toward it. Then he moves one hand toward his body, one farther away, as if he's holding a spear out in front of him. He points it at the chip bag, back at the road, and then at my trash can hideout, and all of a sudden he's watching me, not the other way around.

The Celt sinks into a half crouch, his hands curved as if he's training his spear on my hiding place.

"Hey, son," he says. "Are you watching me? I've told you before. Stay away." He speaks again in that strange language he uses then switches back to English. "Stay away, or you'll get hurt. You hear?"

My heart hammers against my ribs. I get a flash in my head of a news report: a boy missing, a mom crying. I glance around to see where I can run, but there's no-where. Is he going to hurt me? Is that what he means? I grip the trash can. And then a car zooms past and the Celt throws himself to the ground, cradling his head in his arms and swearing.

It's only a car, normal engine whine, normal squelch of tires on the road, faint thud of bass from the radio. It's only a car, yet the Celt is terrified. Guess he would be. They didn't have cars two thousand years ago. He's quivering with fear. At least that's what it looks like to me. I should help him, but his words echo in my head: "Stay away or you'll get hurt." Maybe he doesn't want me to get hit by a car? Or maybe it's more complicated than that. Maybe he doesn't want me to get stuck in his dimension, the way he's stuck in ours, or between his and ours, where you can be captured in the belly of a dragon and never get out.

I race back home faster than I've ever run in my life. He shouts, "I told you. Stay away!" I glance over my shoulder as I hurl myself into our house and slam the door. He's back at the corner of the street, not even looking in my direction.

CHAPTER FIFTEEN

I collapse into a heap on the floor. My brain is
firing like I've eaten five bowls of the crunchiest cereal
ever. What was he doing? The only idea that comes to
me is "stuck." He said he didn't want to get stuck here,
but he is definitely stuck somewhere, between worlds.
By the way he was yelling, he didn't want me to get stuck
there either.

As I'm still gasping for breath, I hear more shouting.
This time it's Grandpa. It's impossible to make out the
words. He cries out like he's in pain. It sounds like he's
dying, like he's being murdered in his bed. I start up the
stairs, and it's only when I get to the top that I hear
his old familiar voice. "Mikey? That you?" It's croaky and
slurred, but it's Grandpa.

"Yes! It's me!" I'm so relieved I could laugh, but then
I realize this whole messed-up night isn't over yet. How
do I explain why I'm dressed when I'm supposed to be
in bed? You see, the rule is, if Grandpa calls out in the
night, I have to look into his bedroom so he knows I'm
OK. He can't check on me because of his leg, so this is
the drill we've worked out.

"Roll call," Grandpa cries. I grab my robe from my bedroom door and throw it on over my clothes. Just as I push Grandpa's door open, I glance at my feet. I'm still in my shoes, and my pants show beneath the robe. I do a last-minute shuffle to keep my feet out of sight while I lean my head around the door, sort of like I'm wearing astronaut boots. A pizza slice of light creeps across Grandpa's room.

"Are you OK, Grandpa?" I say.

Grandpa rubs his head blearily and squints into the light. "Yeah, Mikey. Thanks. I was dreaming, and I heard something bang. Turned into a huge explosion in my dream. The one back at…" He shakes his head. "Never mind. Just glad I woke up. I hate that dream."

"I'm sorry Grandpa. I must have slammed the door." I catch myself. "The kitchen door. I went for a drink of water."

"Just so long as you're all right." Grandpa shivers, reminding me of a dog shaking water from its coat. "You have to shake off the memories, Mikey," he says. "Crazy old man," he mutters. "Since when did I become a crazy old man?" He thumps his pillow and puts his head down again.

I wonder whether all soldiers think they're crazy at some point. Grandpa seems to think he is, but I don't. I mean, everyone loves Grandpa. And the Celt? Will he seem crazy when he's back in his own time? When he talks about dragons on wheels that race three times faster than the fastest chariot? I guess he will. Even his family will never understand. They'll never see what he's seen.

"Good night, Grandpa," I say. He turns over and grunts. As I close the door, I glimpse his prosthetic leg leaning next to the bed where he can grab it in the morning. Grandpa has the right to bad dreams.

I lie in bed trying to get to sleep. I should be tired. My legs ache from running, and they're all jumpy. I can't find a comfortable position, not on my side, not on my back, and my mind won't be quiet either. It churns over and over, asking questions, then watching the Celt in a little private playback of tonight, then asking more questions, then returning to the Celt.

I keep seeing him pull those men from the belly of the dragon, and it doesn't make sense. How can the Celt be both here and there at the same time? He was seeing that dragon he was talking about, for sure, but then he saw the car as well. How can he see both?

I turn over again and thump my pillow just like Grandpa thumped his. Maybe it'll work for me the way it worked for him. He fell back to sleep as I was closing the door, the landing light glinting on his prosthetic leg.

It's the stupidest thing. After everything that's happened tonight, the secret plastic gun stash should be the last thing on my mind, but something about Grandpa's leg makes me think of a hiding place that I've never thought of before: Mom's shoe boxes. She has a whole bunch stacked up at the bottom of her closet. She buys shoes when she's low, she says, to cheer herself up. She's gotten a whole stack more since Dad left. She says she buys pretty shoes because at work she has to wear "sensible shoes."

"Look at me, Jeff," she always says when Dad's at home. "Legs of a chick; shoes of an old mother hen." Whatever that means, it always makes them laugh. Then Mom kisses him and goes to work happy. At least that's how it is when Dad's at home. When he's away, she just seems mad when she leaves for work. And the sensible shoes pinch her toes.

I lie in bed a few minutes longer. The plastic gun stash? Now? Really? But I'm not sleeping anyway. I tell myself not to be stupid. I just need to close my eyes. I think about the Celt some more. How incredible he is. How lucky I am to have seen him. How bummed Kyler will be that he missed him. I'm still not asleep. I decide I may as well look for the guns.

I hear Grandpa snoring the moment I open my door, so I know I'm safe. I tiptoe into Mom's room, slide the closet open as slowly as I can, so as not to make noise, and switch on the small round light inside. It's not that bright, but light enough.

There's a whole stack of boxes. I take a good look before I touch any of them. I need to put them back in exactly the same place, or Mom will notice. I decide to pull out each box in turn, look inside, and then line them up on Mom's bed in exactly the order I found them. Then I'll replace the boxes like a set of kid's building blocks. Easy.

I'm stupidly disappointed when the guns aren't in the first box, or the second. I shouldn't be. If Mom's been smart enough to hide them from me all this time, she won't have left them in the very first shoe box I pick up.

I keep going, unwrapping the tissue paper surrounding the shoes, checking the toes, putting each box on the bed. I say the shoe colors aloud to keep myself awake: black, silver, blue, light blue, purple, yellow, orange (whoa, way too bright!). Some of these are so cheerful we'd have to put on sunglasses if she ever wore them. I work my way down to the very last box. Nothing! I might as well be swallowing dirt, I'm so disappointed. I look at all the boxes on the bed. It's tragic. All this work for nothing.

I strain to see right to the back of the closet where the sad little light hardly reaches. I stick my hand in, sweep around a bit, and my fingers hit something. I get an electric buzz of excitement.

Right at the back, once hidden by the whole shoe-box wall, is a smaller, much older box. It's dark green. The corners have given way, and the lid rests loosely on top. I guess it's been opened and closed too many times in the past. My heart speeds as I open the lid.

There's no stash of plastic guns, but what I do see is a different sort of secret. I glance nervously through the crack in the bedroom door, as if Mom will know immediately that I'm looking and come home to catch me.

I shouldn't look. But I do.

In the box there's a small pair of girl's shoes. They are a bright, happy, shiny red. The same red as the uniforms of the British foot soldiers during the American Revolution. They are the only red shoes she has in her entire collection. They're resting on a piece of dull green cloth. Slotted down the side of the box, there's an envelope.

A voice in my head tells me this is not my business, but, at the same time, I feel excited and curious. I slip the envelope out of the box.

It's addressed to Mom, but Mom before she married Dad. *Miss Christina Andersen*, it says. The address is: *Christina's Bedroom, Upstairs, Home.* On the left, in smaller writing, it says: *From Pa.* The address is Grandpa's house, where Mom grew up. In the top right there's a drawing of a stamp, not a real one. Grandpa must have pretended to mail this letter to Mom when she was small.

I pull the letter from the envelope and find two photos folded inside. They're of Mom and Grandpa standing together in Grandpa's garden. In the first, Grandpa's wearing his uniform. In the second, he isn't. He's leaning on crutches instead, and Mom looks much older. I put them down to look at later because I want to see what Grandpa said to Mom all those years ago.

The writing is big and very clear, like he wants to make sure she can read it.

Darling Christina,

I hope you love these special shoes. Aren't they just the shiniest, prettiest pair you ever did see? I bought them for a very special girl. That's you!

I thought we could play a game while I'm away. Try these on. I think you'll find they are too big right now, but, here's the fun! Let's see if by the time I come back home they don't fit just fine.

You can wear them for me when I come back, and I'll give you the biggest hug a girl ever had from her Daddy.

I love you, Honey Bee, and I always will!

Kisses,

Your Pa

"Honey Bee?" Grandpa called Mom "Honey Bee." Wow, she's kept that quiet, and I don't blame her! This letter is just like Grandpa. He's always been fun.

I go back to the photos and look at them again, more carefully this time. In the first, Mom and Grandpa are hooked together in a big hug. He's smiling down at her, and she's looking up at him like he is the best thing in the whole wide world. In one hand she holds the red shoes. They hang down in front of her, pegged together by her fingers. This must be the picture Grandma took when Grandpa had to leave for Vietnam.

In the second picture, Mom and Grandpa stand in the exact same spot. Mom holds the shoes in the same way, but she's not hugging Grandpa. His crutch is in the way for one thing. She's not even smiling. You'd think she'd be happy because her dad has come home at last, but, if anything, she looks uncertain, even shy.

It reminds me of the pictures Mom takes of me when I have to stand next to some old friend of hers: a lady who knew me when I was two, but who I don't remember at all. That's how Mom looks with her dad. At the bottom of the photo there's one sentence in Mom's handwriting. It says: *I grew up too fast*.

I take the shoes out of the box. They're brand new, never been worn. As I lift them, I realize what the green cloth is. It's a hat. A really worn-out, floppy, wide-brimmed hat like the ones you wear for hiking. Grandpa must have worn it in the jungle. Maybe he was wearing it when he was wounded. It doesn't look like much, but this was Grandpa's. I put it on and stare in the mirror hoping I look a bit like him. I think maybe I do.

Finally, I put the hat, the picture, and all the shoe boxes away exactly as I found them and creep back into my room. No one will know.

When I finally fall asleep, I have a weird dream. I'm crossing a road wearing Grandpa's hat. The sun burns down on my head so hot that a bead of sweat trickles down my spine. I want to run, but the surface of the road has melted into a black mess. When I pick up my feet, strings of gloop, stretchy as hot pizza cheese, glue me to the ground. Then there's a massive explosion. I cover my head as the whole road rocks beneath me, and a blast of heat washes over me. I can't escape, but it's getting hotter and hotter. I look to see where the heat's coming from, and a dragon charges at me with its skin on fire. It's bright red and glowing as hot as the ceramics furnace at school. In a flash I know that Grandpa is caught inside its belly, writhing and screaming for help, and the Celt is trapped inside too, and even Mom. I draw my sword and hack away at the beast, but its armor is so hard my sword clangs against its side and bounces off. The heat brightens the tip of my sword like a marshmallow fork and travels up the metal. I yell with pain and let the sword clatter to the ground. The last thing I remember thinking, before I wake up, is how magnificent the sword is, and how much my hand hurts where I held it.

CHAPTER SIXTEEN

In class the next day, I can hardly keep my eyes open. Every time I think math, my eyelids droop like sagging window blinds.

"My, my! Was it a full moon last night?" Miss O'Brien says. "Because we seem to have two very weary chislers in class this morning." "Chislers" means "kids" in Dublin, where Miss O'Brien was born. She came here when she was little so she sounds American, but she says quirky words every now and then.

I look up sleepily and catch a glimpse of Ryan O'Driscoll's head jerking upward from his desk. By the way he glances around the room, I can tell he's forgotten where he is for a second. I recognize the feeling and grin. He scowls and turns away. Looks like he didn't get any sleep either, but I bet he wasn't chasing a Celtic warrior like I was. Knowing Ryan, he was playing computer games all night. His mom lets him stay up as late as he wants, even on school nights. Well, that's what he tells us. Any other day I'd be mega jealous, but not today.

Kyler winks at me. He's so desperate to get the full story about last night that he can barely concentrate.

Miss O'Brien notices him squirming in his seat and blames the moon again. Kyler's dad dropped him at school this morning, so we couldn't talk. I texted as much as I could but, just like my book reports, half of what I wrote didn't make much sense.

"The bushes, recess," I mouth as if he doesn't already know that's the first place we'll go when the bell rings. As I return to the snaky long division problem winding down my page, I see Ryan out of the corner of my eye. He's glaring at me as if he wants to burn a hole in my chest. What's gotten into him? I know we're not best friends or anything, but he's looking at me like I just threw his cat across the room.

When the bell rings, Kyler and I are by the door before Miss O'Brien finishes saying, "Right, class. It's recess."

"Looks like you've woken up now, Mikey," she says as she lets us out onto the blacktop. I don't have time to reply. We have to snag our place in the bushes before anyone else does.

There's a whole row of bushes along the gym wall. I guess they were planted there to make the playground look better, which is a grown-up thing and really boring. But it turns out they're the best play spots in the entire yard. The really cool thing about these bushes is that the branches grow up from the trunk and curve over like a fountain. This makes a space in the middle, which works great as a den. The kids that play spies use them as hide-outs. The secret "candy munchers" use them as clubhouses. Kids like me and Kyler use them as forts. The only thing is, you have to get there right at the start of recess to claim one. If the girls who play kittens get there first, well, you're lost even when they leave one of the bushes free. I tell you, five minutes of girls doing kitten mewing, and you're ready to tear your ears off.

Anyhow, one of those Celtic gods must be looking out for us today because the "kitten girls" head for the jungle gym and the "spy kids" and candy munchers are playing foursquare. We have the bushes to ourselves.

"Last night sounds epic," Kyler groans, as we crouch in our den. "I can't believe I missed it. Was he looking for a portal do you think? Did he do any weird ritual stuff? Why do I miss all the action? I'm so bummed."

"Me too. I needed you there, dude. I needed your brains!" Which is so true, but I decide to back up and restart by saying how cool Kyler was, the way he convinced his dad he'd been locked out of the house and all. "Awesome!" I say. Kyler blows it off, but he's pleased. I hope it makes him feel better about missing what I have to tell him next.

By the end of my story, Kyler's mouth is hanging wide as a garage door. "He was talking about dragons and women warriors and swords? For true life?"

"True life! And he was terrified by a car driving down the road at, like, forty miles an hour. It wasn't even speeding."

"He's still not used to them, I bet."

"Totally, but how is this whole thing working? How can he be here and somewhere else at the same time? He was seeing a world I wasn't seeing, but he was right in front of me. He wasn't in the Otherworld, he wasn't in a parallel universe, at least his body wasn't—"

Kyler's about to cut in when a tennis ball hits hard against the wall above our hideout and drops onto the branches above us.

"Hey, watch out," Kyler yells.

Another ball scorches past and thuds against the stucco.

"What the—?" I yell.

"You're talking garbage." Ryan O'Driscoll fights his way into our den. He's so mad that when his coat snags on a branch, he rips the branch clean off. His face is red, his neck is all bulgy, and he's inches away from us. He picks up one of the tennis balls and goes to throw it again, which is pretty dumb because we're at point-blank range and all stooped over, but even without room to wind back, Ryan still has the best arm in fourth grade. He could take our heads off right now.

"Stop!" Kyler shouts.

"Know how stupid you sound?" Ryan says.

"You shouldn't be listening."

"You shouldn't be talking so loud."

"If you don't like it, leave," I say. "You don't have to stand by the bushes."

"I can stand where I like. Just stop going on about that guy."

"What do you care?" Kyler says.

"I don't, Turtle."

That's when Kyler points a finger and says, "Just because you were scared of him!"

I duck, out of instinct I guess. Ryan squeezes the tennis ball so hard his fingers go white. "Shut up about him," he says, lifting his arm. Then he turns, pushes his way out of our hideout, and lobs the tennis ball right across the blacktop. Kyler and I scuffle to the front of the bush to watch. It loops up in the air, in one of those perfect arcs that teachers draw on graphs, and disappears over the wall into the street.

"Hey, that could've hit someone," Kyler calls. "It could've hit a car, slammed onto someone's windshield and made them crash."

"Like a bomb!" I add.

"What would you know about bombs? What do you know about anything?" Ryan sneers as he walks away.

CHAPTER SEVENTEEN

That afternoon, Miss O'Brien drops a real bombshell. "Class," she says. "In two weeks we have a day off school. Does anyone know why we are not at school on Tuesday, November 11th?"

I throw my hand up, but Casey cuts in using that chirpy chipmunk voice of hers, "Because the teachers want a party?" The whole chipmunk deal wasn't funny even in second grade, but a few of the girls still titter. Just proves it's good to have friends.

"Hands in the air." Miss O'Brien picks someone else. I'm disappointed it's not me, as I had my hand up first. This question is so mine.

"It's Veterans Day," Eduardo says. Suddenly everyone's agreeing.

"I knew it," Quinn says, flicking his forehead with a ruler.

Miss O'Brien quiets us down again. "Yes, and we're going to do a special project for Veterans Day. So, does anyone know what Veterans Day is about?"

"Yeah! We have a big parade and make floats and stuff, and the best one gets a prize," Casey says.

"Little League won last year," Sawyer shouts. "We got so much candy!"

"That's exciting, Sawyer," Miss O'Brien says, "but that's the Memorial Day parade you're thinking of. We'll come back to that." She slowly scans the room to see if anyone else wants to answer. Her eyes linger on Ryan. He flushes bright red. She immediately looks to me instead. "Mikey, I'm sure you know." You have to trust that Miss O'Brien has seen you. She knows her troops.

"Veterans Day is when we honor all the men and women who have served their country in the Armed Services."

"Excellent! Now, what does Mikey mean by the Armed Services?"

Everyone's in on it now. Hands shoot up and people mention the Army, the Marines, the Air Force, the Navy, and Army Medics.

"And does anyone know why we celebrate it on November 11th?"

This time it's only me. My arm is straight up in the air like a flagpole. Miss O'Brien can't pretend to be fair and give someone else a chance. She has to ask me.

"Because the First World War ended on November 11th, at eleven o'clock."

"That's right, and Veterans Day honors all veterans, both living and dead, who have served in the Armed

Services whether during war or peacetime. It honors all veterans. Memorial Day, though we have lots of fun events as Sawyer remembers, specifically honors those who have died while serving. Do we all understand the difference?" The class nods. "Good," Miss O'Brien says. "So, back to our special project. It's our school tradition that every fourth grade class does a Veterans Day report."

My heart sinks. A report. I could do a great model of a battlefield or draw an awesome panorama, but a report? I'm hopeless at reports. Maybe I even groan, because Miss O'Brien shoots me a look and then changes her expression into an encouraging smile.

"I think you'll all enjoy this because it's not an ordinary report. I'm going to ask you to find and interview a veteran over the next three weeks. We'll present our reports to your parents sometime toward the end of November, so you'll have plenty of time to do a really great job. Remember, your veteran does not have to have been in combat, but they must have served in one of the Armed Services we've just talked about. You can interview them face to face, or videochat if they live a long way away. You could also telephone, email, or write."

My skin tingles from my ears to my toes because the minute Miss O'Brien says "combat," I know exactly the man I want to interview. It's going to be epic. I'll be the only kid in the history of the fourth grade Veterans Day project—heck, I'll be the only kid in the whole world—to interview a live Celtic warrior.

"Yes!" I say out loud. "This is going to be awesome." And suddenly I'm not afraid of the writing part at all, because even if it is hard, and my sentences end up short and choppy, and my spelling stinks, I will still have the best interview ever!

There's a buzz in the classroom as Miss O'Brien hands out the instructions for the first stage of the project. Quinn tells Sawyer that his neighbor just graduated from high school and joined the navy to train as a nurse. He'll interview him. Kyler asks me if he can interview Grandpa.

"Sure thing," I say. Kyler looks super-surprised and pleased.

"Miss O'Brien, can we interview the same person?" Kyler asks. He must think I'm going to interview Grandpa, too.

Miss O'Brien looks at us sitting together, and I guess she thinks the same thing because she says, "Well, it would be nice if you could all interview a different person, but I understand if there's a particular someone you'd like to interview, Kyler." She reminds the whole class we have the weekend to find our veteran. "I'll expect you to fill out your Stage One Planning Worksheet next Tuesday in school."

"You sure?" Kyler asks me.

"Yeah, of course," I say, because I don't need Grandpa. I know he's been in battle and all, but I've got someone way better, and I can't believe that Kyler hasn't thought of him, too. I know we said we'd keep him a secret until we understood how this whole "time travel parallel universe" thing was happening, but Veterans Day is after Halloween. We'll have worked it out by then.

Casey is whining about how unfair it is. She doesn't know anyone in those Armed Services things. And then she says it's even more unfair because Ryan O'Driscoll's dad is actually in Iraq, which means his project is going to be the best.

"You don't know that," I say. "My Grandpa was in real battles, too. He even got his lower leg blown off." What I don't say is that I'm not going to interview him. I should shut up, but I get this rush of adrenaline, and I want everyone to get at least a tiny idea of how incredibly, humongously, five-times-around-the-earth's-crust massive my interview is going to be. "I bet there are all sorts of people we can interview. I am going to rock this project!"

"Mikey! Casey!" Miss O'Brien is suddenly stern. "This is not a competition! This is an opportunity for you to learn how ordinary people make extraordinary sacrifices for our safety and freedom." She drops her voice and walks over to Ryan sitting at the table next to ours.

"Are you all right, Ryan?" She touches his forearm. It's only now I notice that Ryan has gone completely white. "I don't expect you to write about your dad, if you don't want to." I don't know why Miss O'Brien says this. Ryan's project is going to be so easy.

"I can't, Miss O'Brien." Ryan looks around the room as he speaks. "My dad is, like, on special operations at the moment. He's still out there, and nobody knows where he is right now. Not Mom, not Gran, nobody. We can't call, can't email, can't videochat. Nothing."

"I'm so sorry, Ryan. Your mom mentioned that your dad would be out of touch for a while, but I had no idea. That must be very hard."

Ryan shakes his head. He's deadly serious. "It's really big stuff he's doing, and we can't talk about it, or people might die."

"Wow," Quinn says.

"See," Casey pouts.

"Is he behind enemy lines doing covert operations?" Kyler asks.

"Yeah," Ryan says. "That's it. If I interviewed him, I could put him in mortal danger."

"Man, that's intense," Kyler says. "Does he get to kill people?"

Ryan grits his teeth. "What do you think?" he mutters.

Kyler doesn't seem to notice that Ryan has gone from

"Mr. Boastful" to "Mr. Completely Raging Mad" in two seconds. Miss O'Brien does.

"Kyler, that's not the spirit we want to foster with our projects. All servicemen and women have to deal with terrible situations in war. No one revels in killing, but we want to honor anyone who has faced peril, tough decisions, and hardships in the service of our country. And there is a lighter side. I'm sure that the people you interview will have learned new skills, started new careers, made close, lasting friendships, and learned important lessons about life."

Man, I'm thinking, my warrior's not going for any of that. He's just a hero through and through, swinging that sword, spearing dragons, leaping through flames. I make a fist. "Yes!" I say.

Ryan jerks his chair back and walks straight out of the room.

CHAPTER EIGHTEEN

"Are you sure I can interview your Grandpa for my project?" Kyler asks again as we wait in the hot-lunch line.

"Yeah." I shrug like it's nothing. Inside I'm boiling with excitement, but I feel nervous at the same time. I should just tell Kyler about my plan to interview the Celt. Kyler's my best friend after all. But I saw the Celt first and interviewing him is my idea. I'll share Grandpa if I have to, but the Celt is mine.

I guess I must be looking off into space because Kyler elbows me in the ribs. I automatically shuffle up a few spaces in the line.

"He's following us," Kyler whispers.

"What?"

"Ryan. He's following us." Kyler's whisper tickles my skin and makes me want to rub my ear. I can't because I'm carrying a tray loaded with a plate of pasta, a carton of milk, and a container of yogurt.

"He's in the line, dude," I whisper back. "He has to follow us, or we'd be following him."

Kyler nudges me again. "No, look." I would, but his nudge turns out to be more of a shove. It makes my yogurt wobble into my milk carton, unbalancing the whole tray.

"Watch out!" The volunteer mom at the fruit station catches the milk just in time and straightens my tray.

"He's acting real strange," Kyler insists as we hustle to the very back row of the lunch tables in the yard.

Four seagulls squawk angrily as we approach. If anyone is a commercial for our school's healthy lunches, these seagulls are. They're here every day, and no one has to persuade these guys to eat a chunk of cucumber. They eat everything.

"Hey! This is our lunch, not yours," Kyler says. He holds his tray completely level as he kicks out with his leg to scare them off. His Tae Kwon Do lessons are really paying off. I feel a quick pang of jealousy. Kyler got his brown belt about four months ago. I would have been a brown belt too, but Mom decided to cut down on "the fighting lessons," as she put it, when Dad left for Nigeria. I'll never catch up.

The seagulls fly away, but not so far that they can't swoop in the minute we leave to pick up the scraps. As we start eating, Ryan sits down at the very next table. He never does that! A few of the foursquare boys join him to discuss new rules or something, but, for once, Ryan doesn't look interested. He's the foursquare champ, and he likes everyone to know it, but today he just nods, puts in a word or two, and then gets back to staring at us the way a seagull eyes a sandwich.

"See? He looks really mad," Kyler whispers. I shrug, trying to pretend I'm not scared, but I don't want Ryan coming down on us again in one of his rages.

"Let's go play," I say. We eat as quickly as we can and run into the crowd of kids on the blacktop. A few seconds later I look around, and Ryan has followed us. As he skulks about on the edge of the blacktop, he pushes an apple and three cheese sticks into his pocket. No wonder the kid's so big. He can really work the lunch line.

Mom always says if someone looks like trouble, use your feet and walk away. If that doesn't work, ignore them. If that doesn't work, go stand next to one of the lunch-duty people, or tell them what's going on. I opt for phase one of "Operation Avoid Ryan."

"Come on, Kyler, let's move," I say.

We walk over to the other side of the blacktop. It seems to work. Ryan walks the other way, but then he keeps on walking until he's gone full circle and is next to us again. We try it a few more times. Ryan keeps making out like he's not interested, but every time he winds up back at our side. In the end I say, "Leave us alone, Ryan."

He steps closer to me. For some reason he's trembling. He knows as well as I do that the lunch-duty person is way across the blacktop. Rats! I should have gone straight for phase three and stayed next to her. Ryan could do anything right now, and no one would notice.

"Keep away from him," he says.

It's not what I was expecting, and it makes me really mad. "Who?"

"You know who."

"You told us to forget him, so he's forgotten, Ryan. Bye." I cross the blacktop toward the lunch-duty lady. Kyler follows.

I know exactly what Ryan O'Driscoll is planning. He's heard us talking about the Celt, and now he's trying to steal my warrior for his project because he can't use his dad!

CHAPTER NINETEEN

It's Monday, Kyler's doing homework before his violin lesson, and I'm pretending that I really want to be here, on my own, swinging on the monkey bars in Park Two at four o'clock in the afternoon.

Grandpa turns his newspaper over to a new page, shakes it a couple of times to straighten it, and looks up before settling in to read.

"Few more minutes, Mikey Boy, then I'm gonna need a cup of joe."

"Sure, Grandpa," I wave, adding lamely, "This is fun!" I feel like a complete bozo, but what can I do? Tomorrow I have to complete the first step of my report. I need to fill in the worksheet saying who I'm going to interview, how I'm going to interview him, and what questions I want to ask. I've already decided who it'll be, of course. That was easy, but telling Miss O'Brien is going to be a nightmare. I don't even know the Celt's name, where he lives, or how to contact him. So far I've seen him once at the hospital, once on Swinton Street, and once on my own street, but that doesn't amount to having an address.

I swing around and go back along the monkey bars.

Two moms, sitting at a picnic bench with their babies crawling at their feet, check me out as if I'm going to rip their kids apart with my bare hands. When I smile, they look away.

Checking this park is my last-ditch attempt to find the Celt before tomorrow. I tried all weekend, while Kyler was at his Tae Kwon Do tournament. I even talked Grandpa into driving me to the two parks Kyler and I couldn't walk to. Nothing.

If I find him here, I could at least put the name of the street or the park, even if I don't have a number. Ardee Park. That sounds OK. Like a fancy apartment building. I wonder if Miss O'Brien would notice?

I wait until Grandpa is buried in the sports pages and then I leap off the monkey bars to go explore the rest of the park. I make sure I'm nowhere near the babies, but the moms still glare at me. My shoes fill with sand on landing, and I have to half hop to empty them as I make my way to the farthest end of the park.

Ardee Park is a long wide strip of grass at the top of a hill with the monkey bars at one end. On one side there are bushes that are supposed to create a screen between the park and the sidewalk, but kids have pushed through too many times and there are gaps everywhere. The cross street on that side is really quiet. At the farthest end there's a boulder and a street coming up the hill. On the other side of the park, there's a bank up to an old railway, which is now a bike path. The bank is planted with big bushes and tall stands of pampas grass. There's a very tiny stream at the bottom of the bank, a bridge crossing it, and a ramp at one end for the cyclists to reach the path. If you stand on the bike path, you can see the VA one way and the cycle path leading downtown in the other.

The bushes on the bank are pretty big. I walk around them, making my way back to Grandpa, avoiding a few plastic bags of dog poop on the way. Good thing Grandpa isn't here to see these. On one bush there's an old baseball jacket left out to dry. A tree further on has cardboard leaning up against the trunk, and there's a place where the ground is flattened, as if someone has been lying there. Above, hanging from the branches, I find string. People must sleep here, maybe tying tarps or something over their heads. I wonder if the Celt has been sleeping here too, but if he has, he sure isn't here now. I look all through the bushes and find nothing that would specifically say, "a Celt was here." I'm not sure what that would be, but you can bet the guy knows how to look after himself in the wild.

At the end of my search, I'm pretty much back to the monkey bars and I've found nothing except a good stick. I thrash at some pampas grass a couple of times, then a few times more, moving from one stand of grass to the next as if they're Romans and I'm a lone Celt, cut off from my tribe, lost in enemy territory, surrounded…

"Are you ready, bud? Haven't you got homework?" Grandpa's standing up, waving and hollering from the bench. He gestures toward the car. I take a final thwack at a bush, wondering how I'm ever going to find the Celt again.

Grandpa laughs as we climb in. "You always were the only two-year old who could find a stick in a shopping mall, Mikey Boy. Drove your mother wild. Heh, heh."

Back at home I get on with my math homework at the kitchen table. Grandpa, sitting next to me, slurps from his commuter cup as he flicks through the pages of his *American Legion* magazine.

My homework's not too hard, which is lucky because I can't stop thinking about my Celt. I have the most amazing project in the history of fourth grade Veterans Day projects, and it's just out of my reach.

I look back at my math and get the first few problems done right away. Even the harder ones don't worry me too much, although I have to reread my answers and cross out a couple of mistakes.

If I were the hero in a book, the Celt would be looking for me because I owned a special amulet, handed down to me by Grandpa, or because I'd bought a sword in a thrift shop that belonged to the Celt, and he wouldn't rest until he got it back. But I don't have an amulet or a sword. The only thing I can be sure of is that the Celt does seem to show up in our neighborhood, but we can't tell when. My best plan is to keep checking on the laundromat and spending as much time as possible in the parks and out on the street, just like today. Then, if I have no luck, I'll try looking again at night when the fog moves in. That's what I'm going to do; look at night again, even if I am on my own. It's a lame plan, but I feel better for making it. It's the best I can do without Mom, Grandpa, and, just for the moment, Kyler, finding out.

I'm already on the last two math problems. Once Mom goes to work, I'll be free to start on "Operation Getaceltorix Solo." That's what I'm going to call this next phase.

Mom comes into the kitchen and stares into the fridge. She isn't in her uniform yet. "Aren't I the lucky one?" she says. "I swapped my shifts this week so Yasmin can go on vacation. I've got three evenings of staying home with my family, and I have Halloween off, too. There's nothing in the fridge so…how about a movie? Right now! I'll make popcorn. Order in pizza. We'll have ice cream. The whole deal."

"What?" I press so hard on my pencil, the lead snaps. This is a disaster.

Mom closes the fridge, pours herself a coffee and

says, "Maybe we could be really wicked and have three movie nights in a row. We could choose a movie each. Grandpa tonight, Mikey tomorrow, and me on Wednesday. As long as Mikey gets his homework done first. What do you say, boys?"

I'm cursed. This week, of all weeks, Mom gets to stay home. Even worse, this week, of all weeks, she decides to be fun.

"If you want to," I say, "but I was planning on playing outside for a bit."

"But it's freezing," Mom says.

"I know, but I want to play soccer."

"Kyler's at his violin lesson until six."

"I was going to use the garage door."

"I thought you'd like the idea," Mom says. "Dad, what do you think?"

"As long as there's food and a can of beer, you can count me in," Grandpa says.

He's only joking, but Mom gets snippy. "Could you just quit with the beer and settle for some quality time with me and Mikey?"

Grandpa shrugs.

"Does that mean you'll be out all next week?" I ask.

Mom slams her coffee mug onto the counter. "Well, if you both feel that way, let's just forget it."

"Yes…I mean no," Grandpa says. "It's a great idea."

He nudges me. "Isn't it, Mikey?"

"Uh, yeah."

"As it happens I've got *The Dirty Dozen, The Great Escape,* and *Gladiator* from the library. Like the sound of any of those?"

"Yeah!" I pump my fist.

"Well…" Mom hesitates.

"*Bridge on the River Kwai*?" Grandpa says.

"*Platoon*?" I say.

"*Apocalypse Now*?" Grandpa sniggers.

Mom's eyes are as round as cannonballs. "Can't you two pick anything that doesn't have war…" then she catches the expression on our faces. Grandpa and I can't even look at each other without falling apart. "Oh you two!" She's laughing now. "Very funny. But you want to watch a movie? Really?" Her face lights up. I can't say anything but yes. Oh man, this is so not the night for Mom to want to hang out.

We end up watching *Toy Story 3*, which no one really wants to see, but it's the only thing we all vaguely agree on. Forty minutes into it, Grandpa's head flips back like a Pez candy container. His mouth hangs open, and he starts to snore. Mom keeps telling me which toys she remembers from when she was young, which she does every time we watch this movie. Every few minutes I catch myself staring out the window, because I've seen a movement in the street, or heard someone clomping down the sidewalk.

Miss O'Brien said that the Veterans Day project wasn't a competition, but she doesn't know Ryan O'Driscoll like I do. He loves to win. He'll play hard against even the smallest kid in foursquare to make sure he does. It's obvious he's been spying on Kyler and me. I bet he's out there, even now, looking for my Celt while I'm in here watching a bunch of worn-out talking toys. Something catches my eye. I'm sure it's the Celt running past my house.

"Just going to get a drink." I leap up so fast Mom practically bounces off the sofa. I close the living room door so she won't hear me open the front one and stare out into the street. This would be perfect timing for my warrior, but there's no red-headed man. There's only some kid running up the sidewalk with a bag over his shoulder. A kid in long basketball shorts. Who the heck wears shorts when it's this cold? I knew it. Ryan O'Driscoll is trying to steal my Celt!

"Mom," I call, "I'm going out!"

"But Kyler's on the phone," Mom says in my ear. I nearly jump a mile. I didn't know she was behind me. She holds out the receiver. "Something about a project? What are you looking outside for? Here, talk to him. I'll put the movie on pause."

"Kyler, bad timing, I just saw—"

"Hey, I don't want you, dude. Your Mom didn't understand. I was asking for your Grandpa. I've got to talk to him for our project."

"Wow, thanks, good to talk to you, too, friend!" Actually it is good Kyler doesn't want to talk. I nearly told him about Ryan trying to find the Celt before me. I'd have ended up blabbing about my interview. I'll tell Kyler, of course, but not right now. "I'll get him," I say.

Mom is back on the sofa eating popcorn. "He wants to speak to Grandpa," I tell her. "Should I wake him?"

Mom nods.

I shake Grandpa's shoulder, and he splutters into life. "Enjoying the movie?" I ask.

"It probably needs a few more explosions to keep you awake, eh, Dad?" Mom says.

"What?" Grandpa's still confused. "I was just resting my eyes." He looks around and only then understands. "Explosions, did you say? Heh, heh. Now if this was a good war movie…" Mom giggles.

"It's Kyler for you." I hold out the phone. Then I have a brain wave. Kyler's phone call is the perfect cover for me to get out of the house. As Grandpa takes the receiver, I say, "Hey, Mom. Look, I totally forgot we're supposed to be doing this project. Mind if I go to Kyler's house, just for an hour, so we can work on it together?"

"But what about our movie night?" she asks.

"I know," I say. "I'm really bummed, but we have to write it up in class tomorrow. I forgot, and you know how bad I am at that stuff. Kyler's said he'll help me."

"That's nice of him. Thank goodness Kyler's organized, Mikey. Did you write it down in your binder?"

"Yes," I say, "but I forgot to read it."

Mom sighs. "Well, of course, if you need to do homework, you'd better go. But be back in an hour, and take your phone."

I sprint upstairs and grab a pen and a notebook from my desk. Not only will this look good for Mom but I'll need it if I get to talk to the Celt.

"Back by seven forty-five," Mom calls as I run to the front door, throwing on my jacket as I go.

"Sure!" I'm out of the house before she can change her mind.

I hope she doesn't talk to Kyler on the phone, after Grandpa, because that'll totally blow my cover. And if Grandpa says anything about me coming over, that'll blow my cover as well. I hesitate, just for a moment. Then I keep running.

CHAPTER TWENTY

The sun is getting low behind the houses across the street. It won't be dark for a while yet, but it always gets cold fast around here when the sun goes down. The sidewalk already feels like a wind tunnel. I pull my jacket hood up as I head in the same direction as Ryan, toward the VA. I have no idea how I'm going to find the Celt, but I've got as much of a chance as Ryan does.

I cross the road at the end of the street and walk into the fringes of the grounds which surround the VA at the top of the hill. Mom wouldn't like me being here by myself at night. I wander into the bushes, avoiding the broken bottles, go up to the ridge, and look down the other side. There's some old guy sitting on a bench. Another is curled up in a dark green sleeping bag like a giant caterpillar, but there's no Celt.

I go back to the road and look along the street. A bread truck rumbles into the delivery bay of the hospital. I step to one side as the old English lady with the tiny yappy dog walks past and says hello. Her dog sniffs my shoes. "Caesar!" she says, as she pulls the dog away. I sure hope she meant that name as a joke.

Five minutes later, and the Celt is still nowhere to be seen. I decide to check out Big Stick Park to see if anything's happening there. I try to run all the way, but it's too far so I end up walking some and then running some. All the while my brain is churning with the chant, "Come on Celt, let me find you." When I finally reach the park, there are three sugar-rushed toddlers swarming around the swing set. The parents sit on a bench talking about tiring the kids out before bed, but it's the adults who are yawning.

I search through the trees and bushes, but it's obvious no one else is here. There's some cardboard tucked away by the fence, like the cardboard beds back in the alley by the laundromat and at Ardee Park, but that doesn't mean anything.

I leave the park and decide to check out the laundromat instead. On the way I have to pass Ryan's house. I walk to the opposite side of the street and pull my hood over as far as I can to cover my face. His house sure is a mess. I'd hate to live in a place like that. I guess his dad isn't around to fix it up, but why doesn't his mom do something about it? She could pay someone, maybe, but then I remember Mom bursting into tears about three weeks after Dad left. She'd just gotten back from a really bad night shift, and the whole kitchen was flooded with water from the dishwasher. "That's why you've got me here," Grandpa told her, as we mopped up before breakfast. "That's why you've got me." Maybe Ryan's mom hasn't got anyone like Grandpa. Grandpa's the best.

I feel stupid hanging out by the laundromat. I glance through the window at a young guy with earbuds playing air guitar, and an old lady doing a crossword puzzle. A black cat comes up and twines itself around my legs. A couple of cars go by. In a house opposite, some kid is practicing the trumpet. At least I hope it's a kid, because if it's a grown-up, they should have given up a long time ago! The other houses glimmer with the blue light of TVs.

I stare down the alley. There's no fog, nothing but the steady stream of condensation from the dryer vents. If there's nothing happening here, then I'm going back home before it gets really dark. The streetlights are flickering on now, and it's already pretty gloomy down the alley. I take a few steps into it, but I'm too nervous. It was bad enough during the day, but at this time in the evening it looks a mile long, and it stinks as bad as the boys' bathroom at school when the toilets get blocked.

I hear something rummaging in the boxes outside the corner store. I freeze. The Celt could be here, sure, but so could a stray dog. I'm already feeling nervous when the cat at my feet yowls and leaps into a pile of trash. There's a scream, and I think I scream too, as a rat comes chasing out of the cardboard toward me, its yellow teeth bared. The cat is right behind and clamps its claws into the rat's butt. The rat squeals, and the two creatures roll over hissing and spitting. That's it. I'm out of here—at least that's what I'm thinking when a heavy hand lands on my shoulder.

I know him instantly by the strange accent and the smell of beer. "I've been looking for you, Laeg."

I can hardly get my words out. "Who?...Me?"

"Yes, you, Laeg, my friend." He laughs, and that's it. I'm face to face with the Celt, his big hand on my shoulder, his piercing blue eyes staring right into mine. He smiles, and I'm sure he looks like someone I know. Grandpa perhaps. The Celt has the same lopsided, sparkling smile as if he's just about to tell a terrible joke that he knows he shouldn't. Yes, just like Grandpa. And we're face to face! Kyler said he was looking for me. He was right! I feel great. Just great. I am looking into the eyes of a real live Celt. My real live Celt. My friend.

"Now, come on!" he says.

Without even stopping to think whether this is stupid or not, I follow him back up the street as he yells, "Cuckooland!" at the top of his lungs.

CHAPTER TWENTY-ONE

"Where are you going?" I ask as I run alongside him. "Are you looking for the portal to the Otherworld? Can I help?"

"You want to join me? You can be my charioteer, Laeg. Ride with me in every battle. Be my protector until the end."

"Oh, man!" He's going to take me back to his time to be his charioteer, his friend. Of course I want to go. For a split second I hesitate. I see Mom crying on the phone to Dad. I see Grandpa rubbing his hand through his balding hair as he talks to his buds. I see Kyler staring out of his bedroom window knowing he's missed out on the action. But this is a chance in a million. It will never happen again. "Yes," I shout, and when the warrior laughs and cheers, I do the same. I laugh with him because he's not like other men. He's a Celt!

"The men are all asleep," he says.

"Who?" I ask. "It's only seven."

"The other men," he says.

I can't work out what he's saying. Have other Celts crossed over with him?

"They're enchanted. She's bewitched them. There's only you and me to keep the whole of Queen Maeve's army at bay."

"There's an army? A whole army's crossed over?" My chest is ripped raw with fear. Kyler and I have kept the Otherworld wormhole a secret on purpose and now we've let a whole army into our time to ransack our town? My knees feel weak. Seeing my Celt guys in *Romanii: Northern Borders* is one thing, but having them here with their swords and their spears and their blood-lust is another. "What—" I stutter, but the Celt interrupts.

"Don't worry. I'll fight them off one by one if I have to. Single combat."

"You will?" My words come out as a squeak.

"That's my job, Laeg. That's what I'm here for. My duty! My mission!"

"You're on a mission?"

"Yes, here's the first!" I swing around in panic as he darts at a sign standing outside the corner store. It's in the shape of a giant soda can.

"And the warrior swung his massive sword over his head," he cries, "and his muscles bulged and his face grew red with anger as he brought the sword ringing down onto the shield of Maeve's champion. The shield split like a tree stump under an axe, and the man's arm was severed in two."

"That's Maeve's champion?" I'm so relieved I could melt. He's still fighting in realms I can't see. There's not a Celtic army, in the flesh, rampaging through the streets. Not that it wouldn't be awesome, but our town isn't ready for the return of full-scale slaughter and headhunting. "I thought we were looking for the portal to the Otherworld," I shout as he swirls his "sword" around his head again. There's such tension in his arm that I believe he might truly slice the sign in half even though there's no actual sword in his hand.

I flinch. He never touches the sign. He just twirls on the spot and moves on. I look around, wondering what people will think if they see us, but the street's almost empty. There's just one couple kissing on the steps of a house. They aren't looking anywhere except up each other's noses.

The Celt doesn't notice anything but whatever he's seeing in the other dimension. If he were a ghost, I could understand this. They say ghosts walk the same street and buildings they knew when they were alive, even when those places don't exist anymore. There's a ghost Roman legion in York, England, that walks along the original Roman road. If you see them, you only see them from the knees upward because the original road they're walking on is now buried underground. I saw a video online. It makes sense to me. But my Celt isn't a ghost.

He runs ahead and I have to sprint to catch up. "Wait," I gasp. I'll have to get in shape if I'm going to be a warrior's charioteer. I can't help thinking maybe Kyler would have been a better choice. He's much faster than I am. But then I get this incredible thrill that makes me grin wide as a jack-o'-lantern because the Celt has chosen me.

I push myself faster and catch up just as he reaches my street. He runs right past my house. I make sure my hood is up as I follow and pray that Mom is still watching the movie. At the top of our street, I wonder whether he'll turn toward the VA, but he turns right not left.

"Maeve's champion conceded the fight," he says, "and staggered back to camp. The army of the queen quailed to see that the great warrior wasn't even tired." We run on, two blocks, three blocks. The VA twinkles behind us, still like a rocket on a launch pad.

"Wait!" I half croak, half shout, "What about the VA? Does this have anything to do with the VA?"

The Celt just waves his arm as if swatting the whole building away. "This is Maeve, we're talking about. She'll destroy the whole of Ulster!"

"The Hole of Ulster?" I wheeze. The portal to the Otherworld must be the Hole of Ulster, and it's under threat. His only chance to get back to his own time is going to be destroyed by this Maeve, whoever she is.

He's fighting to get back to his own time, right now, even if I can't see it. "But who is she? Why does she want to destroy it?" I'm panting in my effort to keep up. The Celt is like Kyler, so fit he could probably run for miles and never lose his breath.

"Maeve's the Queen of Connacht."

"Why does the queen want to destroy the Hole of Ulster?" I ask.

"Because she wants the bull, of course."

"A bull?"

"Not just any bull. It's the Brown Bull of Cooley she's after."

A bull doesn't sound like a great reason to destroy a portal to the Otherworld, but before I can ask any more, the Celt runs across the road into Ardee Park. He sprints past the monkey bars and across to the farthest end of the park, where he comes to a stop and leans against the big boulder facing the road. "Are you trembling, Maeve?" he cries. "Are you afraid? Send in your champions. I'm here to defend the ford. I can fight two a day. I can fight three. I can fight them all to defend Ulster."

I throw my arms against the boulder for support and lean my forehead against the cool rock face. I don't see a ford. I don't see any champions. I don't see Maeve. I don't see a portal. I don't see any of it.

Finally, when I sense him watching me, I look up.

He grins and I realize that, despite all the dirt on his face, the tangles in his red hair, and the burnt leathery look of his skin, he isn't that old. Nowhere near as ancient as I thought.

When I first saw him at the VA, I thought he was near Grandpa's age, like Grandpa's poker buddies. But those old guys are so wrinkly they look like iguanas. My warrior doesn't look as bad as that. Now that I really study him, I figure he must be the same age as Mom, or even younger. He only looks old because he's been left outside too long.

"Sit here, Laeg, and watch for the next champion. He'll be here soon. I should go to the camp to sleep." He waves toward the bushes on the bank that I searched this afternoon. "But I'll stay here and wait. Maeve will not let me rest for long, and there will be even more soon, a whole host," he says, settling himself down against the rock.

I kneel down next to him, screwing up my face in an effort to think. What I'd do for a granola bar or a bag of chips right now. I need to get my brain firing. He's talking about fighting champions, just like the Celts in my military history book fought duels, one on one, until the dispute was resolved. But I don't know what the dispute is. Is this queen trying to stop him from traveling through the Hole of Ulster? Or is the Hole of Ulster somewhere here, in this park? Is the Celt protecting it? Maybe he's not a traveler after all, but the guardian of the portal.

"But what—" I stop myself. He's already asleep. Grandpa told me once that soldiers can sleep anywhere, anytime. They have to. I guess Celtic warriors are the same. The Celt's head nods down onto his chest. He looks like a toy when its batteries have run out.

I straighten my back and keep watch. On the opposite side of the road, houses are set back behind small front yards. One has a rickety fence and light shines through the slats of wood like a barcode. A plastic bag skitters across the street in a gust of wind.

The moon is shining now, through a thin haze of mist. In its shimmery blue glow I imagine one of Maeve's champions walking up the road. I imagine the moon glinting off the boss of his shield, which is surrounded by paintings of twisting dragons, their gleaming white teeth bared to bite into the legs of the animal in front. The moonlight will make the gold decoration at the end of his belt glow, and his sword will send rays of light searing through the darkness. He could be here, right now, in this parallel dimension I can't see.

But it isn't a Celt that comes along the quiet road. It's two cars, and, in the time it takes for the first to swoosh by, my Celt's up on his feet.

"The next champion in his chariot," he roars, and faster than my brain can even understand, he runs right into the road and hurls himself toward the second vehicle driving up the street.

"No!" I leap up, but I'm too late. The car swerves and one of its front wheels scrapes against the curb. The driver slams his hand down on the horn as his car jerks to a stop. He rolls down the window and yells, "What are you? Drunk? You could've killed us for God's sake!"

The Celt lifts his hand above his head and charges. "Cuckooland!"

The driver doesn't wait. He spins his wheels and accelerates up the road at what seems to be a hundred miles an hour. The Celt stands in the middle of the pavement. He thrusts his arm above his head as if he's puncturing the stars with his sword. "Cuckooland," he shouts again.

I can't believe what I just saw. He's always been afraid of cars before. He could've been killed.

And then my phone rings. Not now! I can't believe Mom's decided to call now. It rings and rings with a stupid submarine-diving tone that I suddenly hate. It takes me three attempts to pull it out of my pocket. The warrior turns and trains his invisible spear on me.

"Go, or you'll get hurt," he says.

"But I can help."

"Not this time," he shouts, just like he did in the hospital. And the way he crinkles up his eyes makes me run right past him, down the road, with my cell phone still ringing in my hand.

CHAPTER TWENTY-TWO

The next morning, Miss O'Brien hands out the Veterans Day worksheet. "I hope you've all been thinking about your projects. By now you should know your interviewee's name, the branch of the Armed Services they were, or are, in, the questions you want to ask them, and how you're going to interview them. I'll give you half an hour to fill in this sheet with the information."

I must give Kyler a panicked look, because he leans over and whispers, "It's OK. I wrote it all down when I called your Grandpa last night. Didn't you ask him, too?" He must think I'm really dumb. "You can copy off me if you want." Kyler angles his worksheet across the table so that I can see it. "Oh and the guns: bookshelf, hollowed-out book, *War and Peace*."

"Thanks," I mumble, "but I've got it covered." I push the worksheet back. I wonder if Kyler sees me blush, because my neck feels like it's burning. I'm still two million percent sure I want to interview the Celt, even though I can't even begin to fill out this worksheet. I'm just going to have to make it up. I curl my arm around my paper, so Kyler can't see what I write.

Miss O'Brien walks around the room checking our work. "Remember, I handed you a list of suggested questions on Friday, but you can ask your own questions, if you prefer."

That's good, because my Celt sucks at answering questions. I don't think he'll do too well with, "Which branch of the Armed Services did you serve in?" I have a feeling that "the Berserkers," won't cut it as an answer with Miss O'Brien.

Last night he said he was on a mission. It was his job to fight that queen and all her champions. I wish I understood what it meant. I can't think of anything to write, so I'm drawing twisting animal knots just like the Celt's tattoos when I realize Miss O'Brien is leaning over me. "Mikey? Are you with us this morning?"

"Just thinking, Miss O'Brien," I say.

She looks into my face and says, "Thinking's always good. That's why you're here. Now class, I'm going to give you fifteen more minutes to finish writing up stage one of your project. If anyone wants to come and talk over their ideas, now would be a good time." Miss O'Brien gives me a special look, as if her invitation was just for me, but Casey leaps up like she's been sitting on a trampoline the whole time and hurries to Miss O'Brien's desk first.

Kyler's still writing like a madman. His tongue sticks

out of the side of his mouth. I stare miserably at question one: *What is your interviewee's name?*

I still don't even know what the Celt's called. All I know is that he's a Celt, uses words like "Cuckooland" every ten seconds, and talks about fighting champions at fords, stealing brown bulls, and fighting a seriously scary queen called "Mayve" or "Maive." I quickly looked up the name this morning on a baby name site, but it just said it was an Irish name meaning "intoxicating woman." The Irish part is good because there were Celts in Ireland, but I had to stop because I was running late for school.

I draw more swirls on a blank piece of paper and stare around the room. It's only then I notice Ryan falling asleep at the table next to ours, his chin propped up in his hand. Every few seconds he flops forward, his eyelids flicker, they open halfway, and then his head jerks back again. Just like Grandpa watching a movie. I bet it was him outside my house last night. Looks like he stayed out all night. I hope he never found the Celt. I hope only *I* did.

Quinn, sitting across from me, closes his eyes and rocks backward and forward imitating Ryan. Casey giggles. Miss O'Brien walks over to see what's going on. "Ryan O'Driscoll, are you falling asleep?" she asks. Ryan jolts completely upright at the sound of Miss O'Brien's voice. A yogurt container slips out of his pocket and bursts open all over the floor.

"Strawberry, if I'm not mistaken," Kyler says in a fake English accent that he's perfected by listening to my dad. The class laughs out loud. Miss O'Brien isn't too happy and neither is Ryan. As he cleans up the goop with a paper towel, he glares at me, which is totally unfair. I didn't say anything. It was Kyler causing trouble, not me.

I get back to work. Because I can't fill in the questions, I write what I do know in one tiny messed up paragraph. The minute Casey leaves the teacher's desk, I stick my hand up and ask Miss O'Brien if I can speak to her.

"So, Mikey?" she says as I pull up a chair. "How can I help you?"

I make sure my back is to the room. I don't want Kyler and Ryan to overhear.

"You're planning to interview your grandfather, right?" she asks.

"Well, yes, but there's another veteran I'm interested in, too, if Kyler wants to interview Grandpa," I say.

"That's nice of you." Miss O'Brien smiles. I shift in my seat because I'm not being nice at all. "Whom else are you thinking of?"

"He's a guy I met at the VA. I saw him when I was with Grandpa." I lean forward and whisper, "He's just amazing. He has big muscles and tattoos, and he knows all about battles and fighting." Miss O'Brien raises her eyebrows. I decide not to say the word "Celt" just yet. She doesn't look ready for it. "He tells stories all the time, and he has his very own battle cry."

"Battle cry?" Miss O'Brien tilts her head slightly and narrows her eyes.

"Yes. He yells the word 'Cuckooland' all the time, and he talks about a queen called 'Mayve' or something."

"Maeve?" She looks surprised.

I nod. "And a brown bull."

Miss O'Brien puts her fingers up to her mouth. "Hmm." She leans back in her chair and rubs her finger along her bottom lip. "This sounds very interesting, Mikey, but do you, or your Grandfather, know who this man is, or did you just see him one time?"

It's a direct question and I hesitate. "Just the one time," I say. "I mean, I've only seen him one time at the hospital. When Grandpa had to go to the ER."

"So you have no connection with this man. He's not a family friend, or someone you can meet again through the VA?"

"Well, no, but—"

Miss O'Brien raises her hand. "I know this might be disappointing, Mikey, but this person sounds very confused. You have to be safe, and your parents should be with you to supervise your interview. You can't approach just anyone."

I feel my cheeks flush. "He's not—"

"Ryan O'Driscoll, get back to your work," Miss O'Brien interrupts, looking over my shoulder.

I twist around. Ryan buries his head in his worksheet. Was he listening?

"Mikey," Miss O'Brien continues, "if you don't know this man, you won't be able to interview him anyway."

"I will," I say, a bit too quickly.

"I don't think so. The doctors and nurses at the hospital aren't allowed to give you his name. So there's no way you can find him again. I'm very impressed that you're so interested in our veterans, but I'd really prefer that you interview your grandfather. It's much easier to arrange and safer, too. I don't mind that you and Kyler share him, if that's what's worrying you. In fact, I think you'll have more fun, don't you, if you work with Kyler? I'd really like you to enjoy this report, Mikey."

"Oh," I say, "OK," but my stomach sinks as if I've swallowed a basketball.

When I get up from my chair, Miss O'Brien touches my hand. "Just a quick thought, but do you think the man is saying 'Cuchulain,' not 'Cuckooland'?" It sounds like "Coo-hul-lan," when she says it.

I shrug. "Yeah, maybe. What's that?"

"*Who*," she says. "Not what. Cuchulain was a famous warrior in Ireland. He fought against the forces of a queen called Maeve. No one knows whether he was a real man or not, but everyone knows the stories of Cuchulain of Ulster. That's the county in Northern Ireland that he came from two thousand years ago, or maybe even more."

"Ulster's a real place, a county?"

"It's a real place in Ireland. Cuchulain was named for a giant dog that he killed with his bare hands, when he was only a boy in Ulster."

I can hardly take it in. The Hole of Ulster! Maybe the portal links us directly to Ireland through the Otherworld and that's why my warrior keeps traveling here. I must be looking off into space or something because Miss O'Brien touches my forearm, to get my attention, leans forward and says, "The dog was owned by a man named Cullen, and it was the size of a pony, fast as a wolfhound, with giant teeth and huge slobbering jaws. It was the fiercest guard dog in Ulster." Miss O'Brien must see my eyes widening, because she says, "I'll tell you what, I'll stop there. Why don't you have a look in the library and find out what happened. There's an old book by Rosemary Sutcliff. Don't be put off by the cover. She was a great writer. Check it out."

I hesitate. "Was he a Celt?" I ask.

"Yes," she says. "The greatest Irish Celtic warrior and champion ever."

CHAPTER TWENTY-THREE

Grandpa's waiting by the lunch tables at pick-up time, talking with the moms about the class Halloween party, which is only two days away. Grandpa likes to come meet me on the days when Kyler goes to Tae Kwon Do right after school.

"I'll bring the biggest, most disgusting Halloween cupcakes I can find," he jokes. "With piles of frosting. You ladies'll hate me, but the kids'll love it. Heh, heh."

The moms think he's joking, and they tell him what an amazing grandpa he is. Only I know he's not joking at all. Class 4B is going to be sick on frosting if Grandpa has anything to do with it!

Grandpa says, "It's good to get involved. I couldn't do any of this when my daughter was a kid. Men didn't in those days, and, anyway, I was in Vietnam." He points to his leg. The moms tut and shake their heads. They all say he's great, and Grandpa chuckles again, "Heh, heh, heh."

He's having such a good time I ask, "Hey Grandpa, can I get a book from the library, like, right now?"

"Sure thing, Mikey Boy. Meet me here in ten." The afternoon sun peeks for a moment through the clouds, and Grandpa leans back to soak up the rays as he carries on planning the party with the moms.

It only takes a few minutes to find the book. It's called *The Hound of Ulster*. Miss O'Brien is right, I'd never look at it normally because the cover's just plain green, but it does have a pencil drawing of a warrior on the front. When you take a good look, you can see he's carrying a mean-looking sword, and he has heavy wrist guards on his arms. Actually, he looks pretty cool. There are pictures inside, too, in black and white. I decide to give it a try.

Miss Halpern, the librarian, says, "Great choice, Mikey. If you like this one let me know, and I'll put you on to some others."

As I step outside, a drop of rain patters onto my coat. Better hurry back to Grandpa, or he'll be complaining about getting wet on the way home. He says he slept out in the rain enough times during the Vietnam War to put him off taking showers for life. He claims he's the smelliest man in California. I know it's not true, but as I pass the boys' bathroom the thought makes me laugh anyway.

I lean down for a quick drink at the water fountain when a hand grabs my coat and yanks me backward through the door of the boys' bathroom. I flail around trying to grab the doorposts, but I slip on the wet tiles. My attacker spins me around. The library book flies out of my hand and slaps against a cubicle door. I lose my balance, throw my arms out to stop my fall, and land on my wrist. I cry out and roll onto my side, holding my wrist against my body. "What the…?" Ryan O'Driscoll is standing over me. He sits on my chest. I crunch up my knees to stop him hitting my belly, but the way he drops down on my ribs still hurts like crazy. "Umphhh," I groan.

Two apples roll out of Ryan's pockets and disappear under the stall door like they're running away. I twist and thrash, but my wrist hurts and Ryan's a dead weight on top of me. He leans over, grabbing my coat by the collar and pulling my face up next to his. For a moment, I think he's going to slam my head back onto the floor, like they do in movies, and it'll hurt like anything. I wince, waiting for the thud and the pain, but then I see Ryan's not just angry, he's crying. His eyes are red, and his nose is snotty right down to his lip.

"Stay away from him," he screams, shaking my head in time with his words. His face is bright red, and little bubbles of spit stretch into sticky strands at the corners of his mouth.

"I found him." I pull at Ryan's forearms, but he sits down harder on my chest so I can hardly breathe. "He's mine," I gasp.

Ryan pulls my head and shoulders even higher from

the ground and shakes me again. My neck muscles strain to keep my brain from being jolted out of my head. "He's not yours." He lets my head drop to the floor.

"Owww." The pain circles out from the back of my head like ripples in a pond.

"Just. Leave. Him. Alone." Ryan jabs his finger at my face with every word.

I tug my head to one side, sure he's going to punch me, but when Ryan finally moves, it's to hide his face in his hands. His shoulders shake. I take my chance, flip my hips, and tip him off my chest into the stall. He sinks against the door and stays there like a heap of laundry.

"Dude, if this is all about the project, then you're taking it way too seriously," I say as I get up.

Ryan pulls my library book out from under his leg and kicks it hard as he can across the floor of the bathroom. The spine bends right open. The pages catch and crumple against the tiles. Then, changing his mind, he throws himself forward as if he's going to rip the book to shreds so I can't use it for my project. I snatch it up before he can reach it.

"That's mine, too," I shout as I run outside.

CHAPTER TWENTY-FOUR

I'm so relieved to see Grandpa again. He's just getting up from the lunch tables and saying goodbye to the moms. He beckons me with his stick. "Come on Mikey, or we'll get wet. It's gonna rain hard any minute, and you know how I feel about rain. Heh, heh."

I have to tell Grandpa. My wrist hurts, my head hurts, my legs are shaky, and I'm completely mixed up. I don't get what Ryan was doing. Yes, he wants to use my Celt for his interview, and I'm not about to let him. I can see why he might be mad, but crying…over a school project? That's so not Ryan.

"What's up, Mikey Boy?" Grandpa asks as we meet halfway. "You OK?" The weird thing is, the minute I have the chance, I don't want to tell him a thing. Grandpa calls it your gut feeling, when you kind of know something, but don't. He says it saved him a whole bunch of times during the war. "Always listen to your gut, Mikey," he says, "and I don't just mean when it's growling for food. Though that's important too."

There's a feeling in my gut that says, "Don't tell on Ryan, not yet." I've no idea why I feel that, but I do. So,

I lie. "I tripped on the way back from the library," I say. "I hurt my wrist."

"Must run in the family." He flexes the wrist that he hurt when he fell, then takes a look at mine. "I'm no expert," he says, "but I think you've just sprained it. Let's get home before we get soaked, and we'll ice it."

The janitor pushes his mop cart out of the gym toward the boys' bathroom. I catch myself hoping Ryan's already gone. I just want this over with. I'll tell Kyler, though. He'll know what to do.

I tuck the battered library book under my arm. "Come on, Grandpa," I say. "Let's get back, quick."

At home, Grandpa scrabbles around in the freezer for an icepack. Bags of peas and tubs of ice cream tumble onto the floor. He insists I have milk and cookies. I say yes to keep him happy. Grandpa believes milk and cookies solve every problem known to man. I'd rather have ice cream.

I end up icing my wrist in the living room. While I'm there, I start on the book. There are twenty names in the first paragraph, and they're all impossible to read. I try to sound them out, but it doesn't work. I nearly give up, until I remember the cookies: plenty of crunches to fire my brain. If Miss O'Brien wants me to read this book, and Ryan doesn't, there must be something to it. I grab a cookie and my concentration improves immediately.

I work out that I can remember how the names look without trying to sound them out, and pretty soon I'm skipping over them and still understanding what's going on. A few pages later, I'm so into it I can't stop.

The first story is about how Cuchulain killed the giant dog that Miss O'Brien told me about. As a boy, he's taken to a place called "The Boys' House," where he learns to become a warrior so that one day he can serve Conor, the King of Ulster. I so wish I were him. Every day the boys learn sword skills, riding, wrestling, hunting, and they get to play a game called hurling, which is a mix between soccer, lacrosse, and hockey. It sounds great.

At the Boys' House, he makes a friend called Laeg who becomes his charioteer, and, get this, Laeg has red hair and freckles just like me. The Celt called me Laeg. Maybe he thought he recognized me. Then I remember what I read about the Celtic Otherworld; that the Celts believed they would be reborn and meet their families and friends time and time again. That's so cool. Maybe that's what he thinks about me—that I'm a reincarnation of Laeg. Perhaps that's why the Celt chose me. But I don't feel like a reincarnation. I just feel like me. I carry on reading.

One day the young boy is playing in a hurling match so he's late for a feast with this guy, Cullen. By the time he reaches Cullen's fort, it's already closed. When he tries to get in, he's attacked by Cullen's fearsome guard dog. He has to kill it to defend himself, but he feels really terrible afterwards because he would never have killed the hound if he didn't have to. Knowing how proud Cullen was of the dog, he offers himself as a guard dog in its place. He promises to stand outside every night, to defend Cullen's fort like the dog did. He kind of turns a bad situation into an honorable one. The other warriors are so impressed by his noble gesture, and his bravery, that they rename him Cuchulain. It means "the Hound of Cullen." And here's the thing—they all chant his name, "Cuchulain! Cuchulain!"

Shivers tickle the back of my neck, like someone is running their fingers through my hair. In my mind's eye, I see the Celt at the hospital. I see him waving his fist at the car. I see him under the twinkling stars. Miss O'Brien is right. It's not "Cuckooland" he's yelling but "Cuchulain."

I read all afternoon and finish the book in bed with a flashlight. The stories are exactly the ones the Celt has been telling. There's one where Cuchulain is trained by the greatest warrior ever, a Scottish woman named Skatha. He learns to leap over the bridge to her house like a salmon leaps up river. She gives him a special spear and he uses it to kill a dragon. The Celt relived all that the night with the raccoons.

Then there's the Cattle Raid of Cooley. Queen Maeve of Connacht tries to invade Ulster to steal a brown bull on a night when she knows all the Ulstermen will be under a sleeping spell. Only Cuchulain and Laeg are untouched by the magic. So Cuchulain stands guard over a ford on the border of the two lands, and he fights Maeve's champions every day until the men of Ulster awake. He gets no rest, and Maeve cheats and tricks him all the time. At one point Cuchulain is so tired that his own father, the god Lugh, makes him fall asleep for three days because he needs the rest. While he's asleep, the boys from the Boys' House wake and fight. They're all killed. When Cuchulain wakes and finds out, he's so angry that he's seized by a fierce battle frenzy. He goes berserk and slaughters hundreds of Maeve's men. No one can stop him because in his anger he turns into a monster, a true monster.

I read this bit about Cuchulain going berserk carefully two or three times. Those Celts loved their fighting, but even they were afraid when Cuchulain saw red.

The last chapters in the book creep me out. Cuchulain kills his own son by mistake. A boy sails into Ulster all by himself and challenges the King. As Ulster's champion, Cuchulain has to fight him. It's a really intense duel, but Cuchulain wins. It's only when the boy is dying that Cuchulain recognizes the ring on the boy's finger.

Cuchulain hadn't seen his son since the child was a baby. He says sorry, but it's too late. The boy dies. The book says that Cuchulain was never the same again.

I take a deep breath and stare at the light from the hallway fanning across my bedroom floor from under my door. I can't keep this from Kyler any more. It's too massive—seventy-times-bigger-than-the-sun incredible.

My Celt is Cuchulain himself.

CHAPTER TWENTY-FIVE

"You weren't gonna tell me?" Kyler hasn't touched a thing in his lunch box and we've only got five minutes till the end of recess. He sits next to me and shakes his head.

"I thought you wanted to interview Grandpa," I say. "I didn't think you'd mind." It's not the truth, but it makes me sound nicer. "I mean it's tons better that we have our own guy to interview."

"You've been staking him out and listening to his stories without me." Kyler takes a slug of water and bangs the bottle down on the table. "I'm your best friend."

"I was going to tell you," I say. "Look, his stories are the same." I push *The Hound of Ulster* across the table.

Kyler pushes it back. "We were doing this together—partners, you and me—and you ditched me." Kyler picks up a piece of sushi and throws it down again. "When were you going to tell me? The day of the presentation?"

"I've told you about him now, haven't I?"

Kyler doesn't look at me. He pushes his food back into his lunch box. This isn't going so well. I knew it wasn't going to be easy, but this is terrible.

It's one of those moments when Mom would tell me

to say I'm sorry, but it's as if hot goop has been poured between my ribs. I know I'm wrong, but it stings so much I don't want to admit it.

Kyler waits. I guess he thinks I should say sorry, too.

I decide to change the subject a little. Kyler will love this. It'll win him over for sure. "You gotta tell me, Kyler, how is Cuchulain living in a sort of parallel dimension? Like how come I can see him, but I can't see the world—"

"Ryan's right." Kyler gets up and swings his lunch box at me, not hard, but enough to make his point.

I duck. "Hey," I say.

"You deserve to be beaten up." Kyler walks away.

>> >> >>

I'm first at the gates when the last bell rings. Grandpa's just arriving. "What's the big hurry? Oh, I know! It's Halloween decoration night!"

I'd forgotten all about that, but the thought cheers me up a little. At least I'll be busy and I won't have to think about Kyler so much. He's really mad at me. Madder than when I dropped his best model spaceship. I took it home and mended it, but it took me a whole week. I don't know how I'm going to fix this fight. There aren't any instructions for how to patch up a friendship when you've tried to keep a Celtic warrior to yourself.

"You seem pretty quiet for someone who's supposed to be excited," Grandpa says as we head home.

"I'm fine," I say.

"Hmmm." That's Grandpa's magic word. Even when you're determined to say nothing, the way he says "hmmm" always charms the truth out of you.

"Kyler and I had a fight," I say. "He's really mad at me about our Veterans Day project."

"Oh yeah," Grandpa says. "I was wondering when you were going to talk to me about that. Seems like Kyler's doing all the running so far. He called the other night, and he's coming over on the weekend. Your mom says she'll cook dinner and he can interview me afterwards. Are you planning on doing yours at the same time?"

"Not exactly," I say. "The thing is…" I hesitate, because after lying to Mom about going out at night and to Kyler about interviewing the Celt, I don't want to lie to Grandpa, too. "I think it's better if we do a different person. He can do you, if he wants, but…" I don't want to hurt Grandpa's feelings either. "Maybe I should do someone else. I can talk to you anytime, right?"

Grandpa looks surprised, but says, "Yes, I guess that's true, Mikey." We carry on walking for a while, then he says, "Are you thinking of one of the poker guys? Gerry has some great stories… Or Jim? We still can't figure out how he ever made it through in one piece. More lives than a cat. He'd give you a great interview. You gonna ask him?"

"Maybe," I say. "Or I was thinking maybe someone from the VA."

"One of the doctors?" Grandpa asks. "Because I'm not sure—"

"No. One of the guys I've seen there," I mumble.

As we reach the steps to our house, Grandpa asks, "Anyone in particular? Because you can't just go around interviewing anyone you meet, Mikey. It's a tough subject for some of us old guys. Even tougher for the new guys from Iraq and Afghanistan. I tell you, it took me years to work out some of the things I experienced during the war. I can talk about them now, but right afterwards… well, that was different."

Grandpa gently lowers himself onto the steps and pats the place next to him. I sit down.

"Mikey, this is hard for me to admit, but I wasn't such a nice guy when I came back from Vietnam." Grandpa puts his hand up to stop me speaking. I remember the photos and shoes in Mom's closet and clamp my mouth shut.

"Listen, I know you love me and the poker guys telling our tales about the war. We can do that now, son, and, I have to say, we do it really well. We tell the same stories over and over, always bigger and better than the last time. We all know how close Gerry was to that bullet; how the helicopter medevaced Jim out at the very last second; even how that darn can of peaches exploded in the canteen and nearly took off my nose. Heh, heh, heh. We've practiced those stories, Mikey. Told them so many times, it's almost like they're not our stories anymore, just tales we tell.

"And then there are nights when we remember one more detail that we'd forgotten: how the ditch smelled of gas; the exact James Brown tune the guy next to us was humming when he got shot; the color of a girl's skirt, in a village, before the firing started. Then we're right back on the battlefield, feeling exactly the same way we did when we were there. We hear the bullets hissing over our heads, we smell the mud, and it's like we're living it again. And those are only the stories we choose to tell. There are still things we don't talk about... Well, you get what I'm saying, don't you?"

I shake my head.

Grandpa sighs. "I'm not good at this, Mikey. What I'm trying to say is that no matter how old you are, you don't escape some memories. You tie them up in a story and you think you've mastered them, but the next time you tell your tale, the memories run away from you. They drag you right back into the thick of the fighting, just like you were there again. It's like a dog on a leash. Most of the time you've got it all tied up, and then one day it runs off pulling you right along behind."

I'm not sure where Grandpa is heading with this, but I stay quiet.

"When you first get back from war it's even worse because you can't tie that dog up in the first place. You don't want to talk about the war at all. You had to do hard things, bad things. Things that, in a war, have to be done. But when you get home, you don't feel so good in your soul, Mikey. You don't want people who've never been to war to judge you and think you're a bad person, yet you judge yourself every day. Most of the time, even when you do tell other people, they don't want to hear it or they don't understand. So, you stay silent and you fight the memories by yourself. That dog runs off with you five, ten times a day, but only you can see it.

"I was like that when I came home from Vietnam, Mikey. Your mom was young, and I couldn't explain what I was feeling so I just kept quiet. That's what we did back then: kept quiet and drank a lot. I'm not proud of it, Mikey. It dulled the memories, I guess. But I was impatient with your mom. I shouted a lot. I couldn't deal with all the small stuff that happens every day. It all seemed so stupid, you see. When I'd seen people die only months before, I didn't care that a pair of shoes didn't fit. I didn't fit anymore. I was difficult to live with and difficult to love."

He shakes his head. "For a while there, I was closer to my buddies than to my wife and kid. How do you admit that to the people who've loved you, missed you, and prayed for you? I'd gone away to war, and for a while I was still away from my family, even though I'd come back. And your mom kept hearing people say we shouldn't have been fighting there in the first place, until she wasn't even proud of me. It was hard for your mom. Really hard. I see that now, but at the time…" Grandpa turns away and rubs his face. When he turns back his eyes are glistening with tears.

"But you're the best, Grandpa," I say.

Grandpa clears his throat. "Thanks, Mikey, and your mom's the best too. She doesn't mean to be grumpy when your dad's away, but she's afraid. Nigeria is a dangerous place—nowhere near as dangerous as war, of course— but they have political problems and that scares her. Look what happened last time someone she knew went to a dangerous place." He taps his leg.

"You don't think—"

"Don't worry," Grandpa says quickly. "Your dad is very safe, but your mom's afraid that when he comes back, it will be as hard between him and her as it was between me and her when she was a kid. That's how people think when bad things have happened to them in the past. If you spend years listening to bombs explode, when you get home, every loud bang makes you throw yourself on the floor and cover your head. It's how you survived, Mikey, and your body and brain won't let you forget it. Guess that's what they call PTS now. Post-traumatic stress, I think it is. We didn't call it that in my day, but we had it just the same."

》 》 》

That evening, I help Mom and Grandpa set up the Halloween decorations. It's always a big deal at our house. Mom says it's because my grandma, whom I never met, loved Halloween. That's why, even when Grandpa and Mom aren't getting along, they make up while deco-rating for Halloween.

They always put out big plastic cauldrons of candy. "Halloween rocket fuel," Grandpa calls it. Grandpa has a beer, Mom sips a glass of wine, and they don't stop until the decorating is done. Grandpa always hides behind a skeleton and makes it talk. Mom always demonstrates the stuff she bought in the post-Halloween sales last year. "The skull lights up purple," she says, "and the rat moves its head when you go by." It makes her laugh.

This year, Mom hides a new fog machine on the steps, and she places two life-sized witches on the front bench of our porch, legs crossed like they're just hanging out. She hides plastic rats in the plant pots, and I hang a giant spider so it hovers directly over the front door. It looks like it's about to eat you. I strap three full-sized skeletons to the railings of our front steps and stick their bony hands through so their fingers graze your legs as you walk up.

"Nice touch, Mikey," Mom says.

She goes back to humming a tune while she and Grandpa stretch fake cobwebs. They face each other on the street, take an end each, and step further and further apart until the white cobweb stretches to double the length. Then Grandpa and Mom give it a final hard tug and walk back together. The cobweb loosens into big fluffy clouds that they pull apart and stretch over the deck.

"Good job, Dad," Mom says. She hasn't been this happy since my dad left for Nigeria. "Now Mikey, let's finish your costume."

》 》 》

It's late by the time I go up to bed. I get into my PJs, but I don't feel like sleeping. I text Kyler to see if he wants to play *Romanii*. He doesn't answer. I imagine him seeing the text and ignoring it. It makes me feel really bad.

I kneel on the floor next to my storage box of bricks

and keep making my model Rome. On the floor next to me, *The Hound of Ulster* lies open at the page where Cuchulain is at the ford and has to kill his best friend, Ferdia, who was one of Maeve's champions. That doesn't make me feel any better. I close the book.

I wish I could talk to Kyler now more than anything. I can't think of anyone else who would understand what was happening last night. I try to come up with ideas to explain what the Celt was doing, why people like Mariko seem to know he's here but then keep it secret and let it happen. Nothing makes sense without Kyler.

When there's a knock on my door, I glance at the clock and realize it's an hour past my bedtime. I scramble into bed, but my light is still on, so it's hardly worth the effort of pretending.

Grandpa comes in, limping slightly after the stairs. "Still up, Mikey Boy? Everything all right?"

"Sorry Grandpa. I was thinking too much to sleep."

Grandpa sits down at the end of the bed. "I hope I didn't upset you earlier. I'm not good at talking about stuff like that."

"No, it's not that." I sit up. "I was thinking about Celts."

"Celts?" Grandpa smiles.

"Yeah." I picture the Celt throwing himself to the ground as the car drove past. "Do you think all warriors get that PT—"

"Post-traumatic stress," Grandpa says.

"Yeah, that thing you were talking about. Do you think they all got it, no matter when they were living, what war they were in?" Grandpa hesitates, so I prompt him. "Like the Celts. They were fighting all the time, killing people, seeing friends die. Did they get it?"

Grandpa adjusts his position on the bed. His stick rattles to the floor, and he leaves it there. He scratches the back of his neck. "I guess they must have, Mikey. And I guess they must have felt pretty bad about the things they had to do and see in war just like everyone else. Maybe they even got concussions from falling off horses and such, just like our modern guys get serious concussions from being near explosions again and again. Maybe all soldiers have suffered similar things no matter what war they were in, but in the stories the Celts seem pretty proud of being warriors, don't they?"

Grandpa pauses, and I can't help thinking about Cuchulain. Yes, he was proud, but he was troubled, too, by the things he had to do. He was a good man, who sometimes had to do bad things, and the fighting made him change for a while.

"I think they were right to be proud, Mikey. I'm proud too: proud I fought for my country, proud I fought for my Marine buddies, proud of the friends I made.

There's no one you care more about, apart from your family, than a friend who's stood beside you in war. People are people. They're pretty much the same all through the ages."

He taps his one good foot on the floor, looks at my copy of *The Hound of Ulster* and then says, "But I reckon there was one big difference. And this is just me thinking now. I'm not an expert, just an old man. But all the Celts and such, they lived and fought and died to have stories sung about them. If you hear good things about yourself, often enough, you believe it, right? If you have stories where the heroes are bigger than life, but they still find war hard, you believe that too. Maybe it helped for other people to tell their stories, to recognize how hard they fought, how hard they died. In those days everyone had a hard life. Everyone was close to death. Maybe they understood war better."

"What do you mean, Grandpa?"

"You come home from war nowadays, and no one understands. You've just seen people struggling to find food, and in the supermarket there are fifty cereals to choose from. You've just seen people terrified for their lives, and here people panic if they don't get a parking space. You've felt the thrill of fighting and surviving, and now the most exciting thing is getting a dollar off a bottle of beer. The contrast drives you wild, and no one turns your experiences into a song."

He looks at the library book again. "How many years ago did that guy live? And people are still telling his story. All his heroic deeds—"

"And how hard it was, too," I say, thinking about the hound, and Ferdia, and Cuchulain's son.

Grandpa nods. "That's what I mean. Is it a good read?"

"Yeah, it's great. He fights at a ford against all these champions—"

"Better get some sleep," Grandpa says, reaching for his stick. "Halloween tomorrow. You'll be too tired to enjoy it."

"And at first he fights duels one on one—"

"Isn't Halloween the night your Celt guys believed all the spirits were supposed to come out from the under-world?" Grandpa says as he reaches the door.

"Otherworld," I say.

"Heh, heh, heh." Grandpa laughs as he switches off my light. "Now, if you were a Celt, that would be one heck of a night to do guard duty."

CHAPTER TWENTY-SIX

It's Halloween, and the whole school is crazy. After recess the kindergarteners parade around the blacktop with masks they made in class. We all line up and clap. One curly-haired kid drops his mask and bawls his head off like it's the worst thing that has ever happened. Normally, Kyler and I would nudge each other and joke about it, but today Kyler's standing next to Quinn, and it's him and Quinn stifling their giggles, not me.

I lean forward in front of Casey Rubens to catch Kyler's attention. "Hey." He turns his back. "Dude, you're gonna be so psyched. I worked it out." I don't care if I sound dumb. No one will guess what I'm talking about. I just have to get him interested.

"What are you, Mikey?" Casey gets in my face. "Some sort of medieval guy or something?"

I dodge around her. "No, I'm a…" but I stop. Kyler glares at me, and I don't dare say it. When we finally join the parade, Kyler partners up with Quinn. I end up on my own.

On Halloween, Kyler and I always go up and down our street together. It's mega fun. One of the houses sets up a whole cemetery in their backyard with dry ice and strobe lights. Another turns their garage into a haunted house. This year, because Dad is away, Mom's asked Grandpa to invite all his poker buddies to dress up as wizards and hand out candy. Even as a normal Halloween, tonight would have been awesome, but now I finally understand what's going on with the Celt, this Halloween is going to be triple awesome beyond awesome. Or at least it would be, if only I could tell Kyler what I know. Missing Dad is one thing, but this Halloween without Kyler is the worst.

As our class takes its turn parading past the other grades, I catch Kyler glancing back at me. For a moment I think he's going to give in and talk to me. "I know what's happening with him," I whisper.

Kyler pulls off his Dumbledore beard and chews his bottom lip. I can tell he's looking at my costume. The thing is, I'd already decided on it before we argued. Now, I guess, it looks like I'm trying to make him mad.

I asked to change my costume last night, but Mom wouldn't let me. "Not after all that effort I put into making the shield," she said. She'd found a big rectangular storage container lid in the garage a few days ago and spent hours spray-painting it blue and adding swirls of gold around the outside. It looks really cool. My whole costume is pretty awesome, but it's not going to make

Kyler like me again. No way.

I can't carry a sword because it's against school rules to bring in weapons, but you can still tell what I am. I have a cardboard helmet and a reddish brown cloak, which Mom made for me when Kyler and I were Roman soldiers a couple of years ago. I'm wearing a yellow tunic, actually a piece of material with a hole cut for the head, and a pair of Mom's red leggings. She's used fabric paint to give them a plaid pattern. I have one of Grandpa's belts tied around my waist, and a big red mustache is stuck below my nose.

Kyler almost swallows his bottom lip then turns to whisper to Quinn. Quinn looks at me and laughs. Even worse, Ryan O'Driscoll catches up with them and joins in on their conversation. He's wearing a black cloak, a pair of glasses and is holding a wand. It's unreal. Ryan is so not the Harry Potter type. He's always a soldier. He's been one every year that we've been at school. Now he actually jokes with Kyler, and they pretend to duel.

"Death to Celts," Ryan yells.

Kyler looks surprised at first, but then he joins in. "Yeah, death to Celts!"

I look down at my shoes. This is not the Halloween I expected.

CHAPTER TWENTY-SEVEN

"Where's Kyler?" Mom asks for the millionth time. She's dressed as a witch and is wedged between the two witches on the bench. It's the only place left to sit. "Isn't he normally here by now? Shall I call Mariko? Or are you going down to his house first?"

I wish she'd be quiet. I don't know where Kyler is.

I've been thinking about him all day, when I haven't been thinking about the Celt, that is. It's the most important night in Operation Getaceltorix. Halloween is the key, and Kyler isn't with me. Because I wanted the Celt to myself, I've messed everything up.

In the hallway, by the open front door, Grandpa empties a bag of pretzels into a bowl for his poker buddies. "Did you put the beers in the fridge, Christina?" he asks.

"That's your job, Dad," she says.

"Let me have a look." The fridge creaks open. "Guess I did."

"The day you forget to chill the beers is the day I start worrying," Mom says. She stretches out her legs and sighs. "I love this moment of quiet before...oh wait, here come the first ones. How cute!"

Twins dressed as peacocks toddle up the sidewalk, their big diaper butts waddling behind them. They have little baskets in their hands. I don't know about cute—they look completely bewildered to me. Their parents follow, sometimes crouching behind the kids, sometimes running ahead, taking photos.

Mom leaps up from between the two witches and skips down the front steps to greet them, "Happy Halloween!" The girl squeals. The boy hides his face in his mom's knees. All the adults laugh while Mom takes off her witch's hat and apologizes. "I forgot, sorry," she says.

"I'll get Kyler later," I mutter while she coos over the toddlers. "When it starts to get dark."

"Sure, honey. Just let me know when you go. Same rules as ever. Stay on the street. Take your phone. Meet back here at nine." I may not have Kyler, but I have an alibi. I'll pretend to go to his house and look for the Celt on my own.

The twins, smiling now, wobble up the front steps while Mom and the parents trail behind ready to catch them if they fall. Grandpa opens the door and all you can hear is a howl. Both kids raise their hands toward their parents to be picked up, and the boy bursts into tears.

"Oh no," Mom says, "now we've really done it."

Grandpa takes off his skeleton hands and laughs. "Heh, heh. Cute little tikes," he says to the parents. The twins aren't sure whether taking off your hands is more or less scary than having skeletal hands in the first place, but Grandpa keeps chuckling and giving them candy.

I sit on the steps for a while, eating chocolate and getting kind of nervous. The sun sets. More and more kids my age arrive, pillowcases over their shoulders, mostly empty, but some starting to get weight at the bottom. Lots of adults are coming through, too. Their kids straggle out in front, running to one house and the next, screaming. It's suddenly all noise, people yelling "trick or treat," guys laughing, moms giggling. A bunch of pirates let off firecrackers.

"Hey, Mikey," Mom calls from the bench. "Could you get more candy from the garage? We're running low already."

"Sure!"

I'm just grabbing the candy from the bottom shelf when Kyler walks in. He climbs up the folding stepladder that Mom used to reach the Halloween decorations on the top shelves and looks down on me. Kyler's so short he never usually looks down on anyone over the age of three.

"That's the wrong sword," he says. "A medieval pommel looks stupid on a Celt." His black academic robe hangs two steps below his feet, it's so long on him.

"Dumbledore? Seriously?" I rip open the bag.

"At least everyone knows who I am." Kyler flings his empty pillowcase over his shoulder and points his wand at me. "Like, who are you, Mikey?"

"I know. I look dumb." I throw him a peanut butter cup from the bag, his favorite.

"Yeah, and you are dumb, too. I thought you were my friend." I'm kind of annoyed, even though he's right, when Kyler says, "Ryan ditched me. We were going trick or treating together, but all he wanted to do was trick me into telling him where you last saw the Celt. Then he ditched me."

"Did you tell him?"

"Sorry," Kyler says, climbing down the stepladder to meet me.

I could be mad, but I ditched Kyler in the first place. "Sorry, too," I say, and with that mushy stuff over I spill everything. "I know why he's here. It was Grandpa who gave me the idea, and the fact that the Celt said it was his duty, his mission, to be here. He's a guardian, Kyler, protecting us from the people that cross from the Other-world. He was a champion when he lived and he still is." Kyler looks astonished. "Don't you see? That's why your mom said they come on certain nights. The people from the Otherworld leak into our world all the time through this Hole of Ulster portal, when bad things are happening like earthquakes and stuff, and guys like Cuchulain have to hold them back. He's a secret hero fighting to keep the balance of history right, all the time. No one can admit this is happening, but it is. The VA patch them up and send them out there again and again. And Halloween is the worst night of all. There will be a huge battle. I know it. It's the biggest secret in the history of secrets, ever!"

Kyler whistles. "Whoa, Mikey, eat more candy. You've got some scary-low blood sugar going on."

"You don't believe me?"

Kyler steps back. "You've been doing a lot of thinking while I've been out. That's, like, a lot to take in."

"I know, but you haven't seen him like I have." I grab the rest of the candy bags and walk outside just as some guy shouts, "Watch out will you? There are kids around."

"Oh wow," Kyler says. We exchange glances.

There's the thud of feet, and the Celt is running up the other side of the street, dodging between children. "Look at them all out here," he yells.

"There's always one weirdo," a dad with green skin and a bolt through his neck says.

"You see!" I dump the candy bags at the bottom of the front steps. "Hey Mom! We're going out right now! See you at nine!" I yell.

Kyler grabs his robe in one hand and sprints past me. "I can't believe I'm doing this."

"Quick or we'll lose him."

"Got your phone?" Mom calls from the porch.

"Yeah!"

We speed up and swerve around a gang of teenagers in hockey masks.

"This is amazing," Kyler says.

"Amazing isn't big enough. We're getting proof of the biggest secret that ever existed," I shout. "It's a zillion times better than amazing."

"It's amazillioning!" Kyler shouts, and he's right.

CHAPTER TWENTY-EIGHT

We're three streets over and breathless. It's too hard to keep up with the Celt, what with weaving through people, dodging little kids, saying sorry to everyone who shouts, "Hey, what's going on?" and, "Careful, guys!" One minute the Celt is right in front of us, running through a whole bunch of zombies, next minute he's racing down an alley leading to someone's backyard. He scales the huge wooden fence as if it's a stepladder not an eight-foot vertical surface, and he's gone.

"We'll never climb that," Kyler whines as he pulls to a standstill.

"I know!" I stop running and bend over to catch my breath. "Bummer!" A fence rattles. The Celt must have jumped over another fence on the other side of the yard.

"We've lost him!" Kyler says.

"He must be going to Ardee Park…Park Two," I add for Kyler's benefit, "even if he is using a crazy route."

We hit the street at top speed, but Kyler, being Kyler, can still ask, "Why that park?"

"He thinks the road looks like a ford. That's where he has to fight to defend the portal," I say, gasping for air.

"What's a ford?" Kyler asks.

I don't even answer until we get to the park. Leaning back against the boulder where the Celt rested the other night, I breathe in the crisp night air and say, "It's a shallow part of a river where you can walk across, and for some reason, the Celt thinks this road is one." I point to the street. "He has to be here. That's his job. It always has been."

Several blocks behind us the VA twinkles like a Christmas tree. Immediately to our right and down the hill, a street teems with people in witches' hats, gorilla costumes, short skirts, and purple wigs. A little girl in a princess dress runs screaming from a haunted house, three middle school boys in football gear crash into each other as they argue over candy, and an old lady pulls a red wagon loaded with free caramel apples. There's a good crowd around her.

"Are you sure about all this?" Kyler crams a peanut butter cup and a mint into his mouth at the same time. I give him a look. "It's a great combination," he splutters between brown teeth. But the look I was giving him wasn't about the candy. It was an "I can't believe you're doubting our Celt" look.

We wait another couple of seconds. "Let's go," he says, "or your mom will freak out and totally ban Halloween for next year."

I shake my head. That's one thing Mom will never do. "Three more minutes. He'll be here. He must have taken a longer route."

Kyler gropes around in his pillowcase. "It's eight thirty," he says, "and I've only got five pieces of candy. This will be the worst Halloween ever, unless we hit the houses hard. Now!"

"We're looking for the Celt, Kyler, not candy."

Kyler searches through his pillowcase. "It's Halloween, Mikey! Once a year!"

"A Celt is once a century, once a lifetime," I say. "Once ever!" I get so worked up about it that I yell, "Cuchulain!" into the night sky. The stars seem to twinkle more brightly when I do. Kyler laughs and joins me. We climb onto the boulder and shout, "Cuchulain! Cuchulain!" until our cheeks shake and our faces burn.

A grim reaper dude, a skeleton, and three girls in devil horns and scary high heels wave at us from across the street.

"They want more candy," one of the girls says.

"Yeah. More candy!" the other girls giggle.

The grim reaper grabs a chocolate bar from his pillowcase and throws it across the road. Then the skeleton does the same thing. The girls egg them on.

"More candy! More candy!" they shout.

Kyler howls, "Cuchu-candy! Cuchu-candy!"

The grim reaper throws a whole handful of hard candies. The skeleton copies, and suddenly we're in a hail of candy just like the Memorial Day parade.

"Awesome!" Kyler laughs as a piece of taffy pings his arm and a box of mints bounces off his head.

"Got him," the skeleton yells.

"Aww, poor little guy," the girls say. "Don't hit him!"

"No, keep going," Kyler begs. "Here, get me here." He points to his chest.

So the guys keep at it. Hard candies smash into pieces on the curb in front of us. Chocolate bars thud onto the road. Small boxes explode, scattering gummies like fireworks.

"Thanks, guys!" Kyler yells.

"Sooo cute." The girls coo until they get bored and then totter down the road, waving goodbye. The guys follow, still arguing about which one was most on target.

Kyler leaps down from our rock, picking up candy like a pecking hen. "This is great!" he says, stuffing his pillowcase. "I'll be stocked up until Easter!"

I jump down after him, and I'm just about to snatch a bar from right under his nose when I'm distracted by shouting.

"Laeg! Laeg, my friend!" the Celt roars as he runs down the bank from the bike path and into the open. "What's happened? I've been asleep. Was I bewitched?

I must be ready for the next champion." He slaps me on the back then points to Kyler. "Who's that? The boy, who's the boy?"

Kyler drops his pillowcase. "Me?" His voice is high and wobbly. He sidles next to me, his shoulder touching mine.

"It's OK, Cuchulain. He's my friend." The Celt doesn't correct me when I call him Cuchulain. This is the best night of my life.

"From the Boys' House? But where are the others?" he says.

"You are Cuchulain, aren't you?" I say because I need to hear him say "yes, you're right." And then the world will be more incredible than any book, or movie, or video game I've ever played.

He doesn't answer. He just looks at the broken candy scattered over the road. "They're dead," he says. "All dead! Look how their teeth and bones collect in the ford." The Celt grips his hands behind his head. "I should've been here to stop it!" He rocks backward and forward on his heels, bringing his elbows together in front of his face.

"He's stuck in his parallel universe again, Kyler," I mutter.

"Mikey," Kyler whispers. "Let's go!" He looks scared, not excited.

I ignore him and make myself think, picturing the

pages of *The Hound of Ulster*, remembering the illustrations. I've got it. This is the story of the slaughter of the boys from the Boys' House. "Cuchulain," I say, "it's not your fault that the boys were killed. You were tricked into sleeping. They woke while you slept."

"It was Odin," he says.

I shake my head, puzzled. How can he make this mistake? "No, it was Lugh—you know, your father. Odin is a Viking god."

"No." The Celt screws up his face like he's trying to remember something. "Task Force ODIN: Observe, Detect, Identify, and Neutralize. We need them to win back the roads."

"Win back the ford you mean?"

"The roads," he says. "We need their help to understand what the enemy are planning, who's involved. It's air surveillance we need."

I can't even imagine what he means by air surveillance, but this is proof that the Defense Department is talking to him, helping him out in secret, discussing tactics, giving him new English words to use.

"Otherwise everyday it's the same. We patrol. We clear. A new one comes," he says.

"A new champion?" I'm trying to make sense of what he's saying, but he's lost again in his parallel dimension.

The Celt shakes his head. He wrestles a bottle from

his pocket and takes a huge swig. "And then the warrior transformed, and they knew that he was lost to the battle frenzy, hideous and ugly." The forces of Halloween are really gripping him now. "Even Laeg, his closest friend, knew nothing could be done to save the warrior except to stay clear and let the battle fury run its course."

Wow! I'm thinking, even as Kyler pulls me away by the sleeve. "Come on, Mikey."

I wrestle him off. "No, Kyler, this is it. The start of the biggest battle ever, when he avenges the death of the boys. He attacks all of Maeve's forces. If they try to cross now, he'll defeat them all!"

Kyler shakes my arm really hard. "We need to go!" He drags me away.

I push him off. "No, Kyler. We have to see this. This is it! This is the moment!"

"Every joint in the warrior's body cracked and shook," the Celt cries. "He was like a tree in a storm whipped into different shapes until the muscles under his skin rippled, and twisted, and changed places. His feet twisted backward, his knees bent like a dog's. He sucked in one of his eyes until it was so deep in his skull that it was lost. The other eye rolled from its socket and swung loose across his cheek..."

The Celt is going berserk now, distorting his body, his voice raw and hoarse. He's incredible. Some teenagers run down the steps of the nearest house on the corner.

"Look at this guy!" they yell.

The Celt is immediately alert. "Stay back." Then he shouts a command in another language just as a car appears along the street from the left. Rap music spills out of the windows, bass booming. Guys in the back slam into each other with the beat. The driver has one hand on the steering wheel. He thumps the other down on the car horn...

As the Celt runs right into the road.

As I yell, "Cuchulain! Stop! It's a car!"

As Kyler screams.

There's a squeal and a smell of burning rubber. The car skids across the road. The Celt leaps to one side. Roaring "Cuchulain," he slams his forearm down on the back of the trunk as the car skids past. The metal pops where the Celt dents it.

The car screeches to a stop, so it's sideways in the road, and the two rap dudes pile out of the backseat. "No one beats up on my car!" the driver shouts, flinging open his door.

It's three against one, but the Celt isn't afraid. He howls his battle cry and faces them. "So Maeve sends three against one. Is that it? To fight the champion?"

Across the road, parents pick up their children and move away. A man dressed as Count Dracula calls 911.

"Police? Police? There's a fight! Twenty-ninth and Ard-ee. A homeless man. Maybe drunk. Nearly got hit. He's trying to stop cars…yes, stop them in the road…and the driver's retaliating. No, nobody's armed."

I run into the road waving at the rappers and at Count Dracula, shouting, "It's OK, he's a Celt," and even as I say it I hear how crazy it sounds. Then I hear another voice, a boy's voice.

"Dad!" he yells. "Dad!"

A boy runs into the road. He's wearing an academic gown and has a large bag hanging from his shoulder. It's not a trick-or-treating bag, but a grocery tote. As he trips down the curb, a container of yogurt drops out and rolls at his feet.

The rap guys freeze. They look from me, to the Celt, to the boy.

Dad? I think. *Dad?*

Because the boy is Ryan O'Driscoll.

CHAPTER TWENTY-NINE

The rappers are totally freaked. "Whoa, it's OK, dude." They step back. "Chill!"

As we stare at Ryan, my first thought is that I can't believe he's outsmarted me. He's faking me out, claiming the Celt is his dad, so he can get to him first. I feel red-raging mad, just for a second, and then realization burns up my throat like barf.

I remember Ryan in class, his pockets stuffed with food, spilling yogurt on the floor. Ryan falling asleep on the very same mornings that I did at school. Ryan telling me to stay away from the Celt and trying to rip up *The Hound of Ulster*. Ryan screaming, "You don't know anything."

I didn't. I didn't know a thing!

And that's when someone sets off more firecrackers down the street. The Celt flinches and then his eyes blaze. He looks directly at Ryan. "He's the trigger, dammit! Can't you see? They're using a boy!"

The rap dudes take their chance and run back to the car. "Get in," the driver orders. He revs his engine and takes off, tires squealing on the road, while the teenagers on the sidewalk record everything on their phones.

But I can't run away, and Ryan doesn't run either. He walks slowly toward his dad, his eyes glistening with tears. "Dad," he whispers. "Dad." His dad backs away. And there's the truth, right in front of me. Ryan has been trying to find his father, all this time.

It's as if I've taken off sunglasses and the world is a different color. This man I've been following is not Cuchulain. He's not a Celt. He's Ryan's dad. He's not in Iraq. He's a veteran, back at home. And I've made up all sorts of stupid crazy stories. Not one was right. Ryan also made up stories, to hide the fact that his dad's on the street. None of them was the real story.

I get it now. I get why Ryan beat me up, why he's hated me all this time. His dad is the big secret. And I nearly blew everything apart, like a bomb.

"Put the bag down," the Celt orders as Ryan keeps walking forward. "Put. It. Down. And keep back. Keep back."

"It's food, Dad." Ryan slowly moves his bag to the front of his body. His hands are shaking. "Just food."

"Put the bag down. I'm gonna shoot. Dammit, kid, I have to shoot!"

A bus labors up the road and, for a second, no one on the other side of the street can see what we see. Ryan's dad puts his arms up as if he's holding, not a spear—I see that now—but a gun. He points at Ryan. Ryan screams.

There's no gun, but the instinct is the same. I shout, "Not this time!"—the very same words he used in the VA —and in that split second my Celt collapses to his knees.

"I can't do it again! I can't shoot him. He looks like my son," he sobs.

Everything slows down. He looks at his hands, stretching them out in front of him. He looks from Ryan, to me, and back to Ryan again. I fall to my knees next to him. "He *is* your son. It's Ryan, your son. And you are… you. We're in California. We're safe!"

Ryan draws close to his dad. He wraps around him, as curved as a question mark, and hugs him tight.

Across the road, as if in another world, people on the sidewalk begin to talk and even laugh. The teenagers wander back down the street staring at their phones. Behind us, the fluorescent lights flicker in the towering VA, and the stars in the night sky glimmer like pin pricks in black construction paper.

"I'm opening my bag," Ryan says, stepping back and pulling the tote off his shoulder. "There's nothing in it, Dad, except food. I've been trying to bring you food," Ryan turns his gaze on me. "For weeks."

Ryan's dad shakes his head. "He looked just like you." He presses his fingers into his eyelids. Tries to talk again. Stops and waits.

We wait too. We wait for Ryan's dad's story, but he can't talk and the only words we hear are Kyler's as he breaks in between us.

"The police," he says in a wobbly voice. He points across the road where two cars are driving up the street to the intersection. "We're in so much trouble."

Ryan's eyes are wide, and he's shaking. "Oh, no!" He grabs his dad's hand and pulls. "Come on, Dad! You can't get arrested. You just can't. We've gotta get out of here."

"Wait," I say to Ryan's dad.

"Are you trying to get him arrested?" Ryan shouts.

"No!" To be honest right now I don't know what I'm doing. "But you can't stay on the streets!" The Celt looks at me. "Well, you can't."

The officers get out and look around. Count Dracula approaches. "Over there. The guys in the car drove off."

"They'll take you away, Dad," Ryan pleads.

"And if we run, won't it look worse?" I say.

Ryan's dad mutters, "I don't know. I don't know." And I don't know what they'll say or do, either. Whatever we've done, I can't help feeling it's wrong, but running feels wrong too. I've never been so scared.

"No one was hurt," Count Dracula is saying, "but he was acting really strangely…yes…in the middle of the road, challenging cars. Near kids."

Ryan's dad is a veteran, like Grandpa, not a Celt.

The idea comes to me in an instant.

"Kyler, get Grandpa. Now!"

Kyler hesitates for a second, looking confused. "He'll help," I insist, and Kyler gets it. He runs like the wind toward the monkey bars before the police even realize he's disappeared.

"Where's he going?" Ryan blurts, but I speak directly to his dad.

"My Grandpa's at home right now, with his buddies, just down the street. They're Marines, sir. Veterans. Every single one was in Vietnam. Just wait for them. Please! They'll understand. They'll know what to do."

"No, Dad," Ryan urges. But it's already too late. The officers are walking across the street. One is really tall and strong, the other more wiry and skinny. They both look determined and in control. "Everything OK over there, boys?" they call.

"Trust me, Ryan." I take Ryan's dad's hand. It's hot and clammy. I swear I feel his pulse racing. Ryan chews his bottom lip then takes his dad's other hand.

The police walk slowly and calmly across the grass to meet us. "Everyone OK?" they ask again.

I just have to delay until Grandpa arrives.

"Yes, sir," I take a step forward. "We're all fine. We're just waiting for Grandpa. Ryan and I are just fine and Ryan's dad is fine, too. My Grandpa's coming for us. We only live down the street."

The officers look past me. "And you're OK, son?" they ask Ryan.

"Yes, sir," Ryan says.

"Sir, have you been drinking?" One of the police officers approaches Ryan's dad. "We hear you were in the road earlier."

"I got confused, officers. I'm sorry, but I'm OK now," he says, quietly.

"Your name, sir."

"O'Driscoll," Ryan's father says. "Liam O'Driscoll."

"Do you have ID?"

"My driver's license, I think." Liam looks worried as he fumbles through his pockets, swaying slightly. He finds nothing. Searches again. Ryan screws the hem of his shirt in his hand.

"You all out enjoying Halloween?" the tall officer asks as we wait. And it's only then that I wonder what we must look like. We look weird it's true, but not *that* weird seeing as it's Halloween. I just have to keep them talking.

"That's right," I say. "Ryan's dad and I are Celts, you know, those guys who fought the Romans."

"Cool," the tall officer says. Liam's still pulling stuff out of his pants' pockets. They're plaid PJ bottoms. Why didn't I see that?

"And Ryan's Harry Potter. And my friend Kyler was

Dumbledore, so…we…like match, in pairs, and my Grandpa and his buddies are wizards. They'll be here soon," I add.

"Here," Liam says suddenly, handing over a yellowed, curved piece of plastic. "Here it is."

The officer nods. "Mind if we check?"

Come on, Grandpa, I'm thinking. *Come on.* The tall officer takes the card, walks to his car and radios in. He leans into the open car window with one elbow on the sill as if he's already tired and knows the evening has only just begun. The radio crackles. He listens, talks, and listens some more.

Every time a car goes past, Ryan looks at his dad. I look for Grandpa. The skinny officer makes conversation.

"Have you been to a party, sir? Or are you going to one? You're not intending to drive?"

Hurry Grandpa, please hurry. If Ryan's dad gets arrested, it'll be my fault. If Ryan's dad gets arrested, he'll be taken from Ryan again. If Ryan's dad gets arrested…

The tall officer finishes his conversation on the radio, and makes some sort of hand signal to his colleague as he walks back. This is it. They're going to arrest him. I can't think of anything else to say, anything else to do. And that's when Grandpa and Gerry, one of his buds, drive around the corner.

"Grandpa!" I yell. "See," I say to the officer, "there's

Grandpa, just like I said."

They park on the cross street and Grandpa gets out of the passenger side as fast as he can, heaving himself out with one strong arm, struggling with his stick, and knocking his wizard hat from his head.

"All right, Mikey Boy?" Grandpa waves. "Are you all right, son?"

He walks across the grass to meet the tall officer, and they shake hands. "Marty!" the officer says, clapping Grandpa on the back.

"Steve," Grandpa says, "how are you? I haven't seen you at the Legion since you were Honor Guard at the Memorial Day Parade. Where've you been?"

"Busy, Marty. Coaching two basketball teams and my oldest is doing college tours, you know?"

Grandpa keeps walking alongside the officer, limping over the bumpy grass. "Is everything all right here?" he asks, "with my grandson and his friends?"

The officer hesitates, as if wondering what he should say. "Look, Marty, we've had some complaints," he says, "about public drunkenness, and endangering cars on the street."

"But, everyone's calm and cooperative now?" Grandpa says.

The tall officer approaches Ryan's dad. "Yes, but we got a report—"

"But he has an appointment," I break in. I probably shouldn't, but I do. "Tonight…at our house…with Dr. Mariko Curtis."

Steve looks to Grandpa. Liam and Ryan just look confused.

"That's right," Grandpa quickly fills the silence. "With Dr. Mariko Curtis, from the VA. My friend here has seen…how many tours?"

Grandpa walks up to Liam like he's meeting us in the schoolyard, holding his arm out in greeting.

"Three," Ryan cuts in. "Three tours."

"That's right, son. Isn't it?" Grandpa shakes Liam by the hand and gives him a friendly pat on the shoulder. Then he whispers, "Semper Fi. We'll straighten this out."

"Well, I know something about that," Steve says.

The officers back off a little to talk. Grandpa joins them. "Maybe you could follow us, Steve, and discuss this with the VA doc?" he suggests.

The policemen talk in low tones and exchange glances. "That's reasonable," Steve says, finally. "We'll follow you, Marty."

We make our way slowly toward the car, me on one side of Ryan's dad, Ryan on the other, while Grandpa chats with the officers. There's no one like Grandpa.

The minute we're in the car and Gerry starts to drive, Grandpa calls Mariko. "Meet us outside the house," he says as he ends the call. Then he relaxes back in his seat. "There's no need to say anything right now; not until we're home."

CHAPTER THIRTY

Mariko is waiting outside our house with Kyler when we arrive. The police hover outside, talking to her. They look concerned, but not angry. They listen and nod and phone in on their radios again.

Grandpa escorts Liam up the front steps and into the kitchen where the rest of Grandpa's buddies are waiting. They shake his hand and say, "Semper Fi."

"Welcome," Mom says.

Ryan's dad looks confused and sad. Ryan stands next to him, his hand on his dad's shoulder. Kyler and I don't know where to stand, or what to do now.

When Mariko hurries in she just says, "It's all right. They understand."

Grandpa introduces her to Liam. "Mariko is a good friend and a great doctor. You can trust her, son." Mariko smiles. Grandpa moves so she can sit down next to Ryan's dad. She starts assessing him the way she did Grandpa at the ER. Her voice is quiet and calm.

Mom brews coffee at the kitchen counter. She catches my eye and points to Kyler. We walk over to see what she wants. "Boys, will you empty the last bags of candy into the cauldron on the porch and leave it at the bottom of the steps? The trick or treaters can help themselves. We don't need to be disturbed right now."

Outside, kids are still running up to houses and having fun. We dump the candy just like Mom told us to, putting a few pieces in our pockets.

"Are you OK?" Kyler asks as we walk back up the steps to the front door.

"I got everything wrong." I feel sick just saying it.

Kyler shrugs.

Mom is by the door as we come back inside. She switches the porch lights off. "Now, take Ryan upstairs," she whispers. "This might take some time."

"No!" Ryan overhears. "I don't want to go. He's my dad."

"It's OK, Ryan," Mom says. "I'll call your mom."

"You can't," Ryan snaps. "She thinks he's staying with friends."

Ryan's dad cradles his head in his hands and leans forward so we can't see his face. It's as if he wants to curl up into a ball and never uncurl again.

"She'll understand. Really she will," Mom says. "You boys have done the right thing."

"You don't know anything—" Ryan shouts. His dad catches his hand. They look at each other. Ryan glares and wriggles out of his father's grasp. He can't run out the front door because we're blocking the way, so he bolts upstairs instead. My mom chases after him. "Ryan!"

As they disappear, I hear her say, "I'm the kid of a veteran. I have some idea…" Ryan's footsteps thump up the stairs. My door closes. Mom asks to be let in and after a while the door opens and closes again. Kyler and I don't know what to do. We can't go to my room right now. We can't really sit in the kitchen, either. So we sit at the bottom of the stairs and wait.

We hear the men talking in low whispers and then Liam lets out a sob and speaks. "It was a wedding party. People were all dressed up on the streets, like tonight. It was my third tour in Iraq. I was in the Reserve by then, but I got redeployed. I didn't know if I could hold out. I was always on edge, always jumpy. Someone set off fireworks. I smelled cordite and then a boy approached with a bag of candies for the wedding. He was just a kid. We're supposed to keep kids away from our patrol, but I let him get up close. Too close. He pulled out a cell phone.

"The guys in my patrol are shouting, 'Cell phone! Cell phone!' I yell at the kid, but he doesn't put the phone down. At that point I'm supposed to shoot, but I couldn't because he reminded me of my son and my heart ached. And then the kid hit the button and the Humvee went up in flames, and I shot the kid, and…" He pauses.

"I was supposed to protect the guys inside, but they got blown up. I dragged them out, but it was too late."

Kyler gasps. I hold my breath. He had no choice. There was no right thing he could do. We hear Grandpa and his buds talking to Liam, sharing, and then Mom comes out of my bedroom and tells us to come up and keep Ryan company. Mariko is already making phone calls in the kitchen.

Ryan's standing with his back to us in one corner of my room. He rests his forehead against the wall. Kyler looks at me. "What are we supposed to do?" I mouth. Kyler shrugs. I take a step toward Ryan, but I get scared, so I kind of turn it into another move and sit on the floor instead. I rearrange some Roman cavalry soldiers that I left under my desk. Kyler stretches out on my bed, pretending to read a book. I feel so uncomfortable I could split right out of my skin. Ryan hates me, even though he isn't saying a thing. Yesterday I didn't care whether he hated me or not. Now, I do.

Below, the grown-ups talk. Sometimes Ryan's dad shouts, sometimes he cries. We can't hear clearly, but every time there's a shout, Ryan tenses and his hands ball into fists. Finally, he turns and slides down until he's sitting with his elbows on his knees, his head resting back against the wall. His mouth is a tight hard line.

I did the right thing, I tell myself. But maybe I didn't.

Maybe I just got Ryan and his dad into a whole lot of trouble. My stomach churns at the thought of it.

"He didn't want to risk hurting you," I whisper. "That's why he hid from you." I don't dare look at Ryan. I twirl a Roman soldier around on the floor. There's no answer. "Kyler's mom will look after him. She always helps Grandpa." I glance up, and the way Ryan returns my gaze makes me wish I'd never said a thing.

The doorbell rings, and a woman calls out. It's an indescribable noise caught between screaming and crying. "Mom!" Ryan leaps up and runs to the bedroom door. He grasps the handle and I don't know whether he means to fling the door open or barricade himself in. "She's gonna kill me."

"No, she's not." I might be wrong, but I stand up and keep going. "You wanted your dad to stay near you. We all understand that. She will too. My dad's in Nigeria, and I sure don't want him to be there. I mean it's not the same as your dad being at war," I say really quickly. "It's not the same as your dad going to Iraq again and again and each time worse…" I take a sidelong look at Ryan expecting that he'll be so mad that he'll want to punch me, but he doesn't move. Then I feel a burning inside my gut and the words topple out of my mouth, "But Dad's been away for five months, and he's going to be there another nine, and I miss him. Mom's horrible when he's away. She gets so stressed she goes ballistic even if I just leave a book on the floor or forget my homework."

When I've finished, I feel so dumb I just look down at my feet. Kyler turns a page. Then Ryan says, "My mom can't get through a single day without yelling, and if she's not yelling she's crying or sleeping on the couch. She never goes out anymore. It sucks." That sums it up.

"Yeah, it sucks."

There's more crying downstairs. Ryan draws in a breath. "And your dad's like Cuchulain," I say. "He did the right thing, and he did the wrong thing, both at the same time. He had no choice."

Ryan's eyes glisten and he wipes his face with the back of his arm.

"Forget that," Kyler says over the noise.

"What?" I say, taken totally by surprise.

"Let's do something fun. Let's look for the plastic gun stash."

That's the last thing on my mind right now. I can't believe Kyler would say such a dumb thing, but Ryan says, "What gun stash?" and looks almost interested.

I go with it. "Great idea," I say.

Ryan's completely in the dark so I fill him in. When we get to the bit where Mom used black markers to erase the gun pictures on the boxes, Ryan laughs out loud. Even though he has to wipe his face again and his voice is still shaky, he says, "Dude, your mom's crazier than mine!"

"Yeah," I say. "It sucks."

"Sucks," he echoes.

"Mega sucks," I say.

"Mega, mammoth sucks," Kyler says.

"Mega, mammoth, tyrannosaurus sucks," Ryan says. He gets the game right away, and wins. Kyler and I high five.

"The guns have to be in a secret compartment," Kyler says, "like under the floorboards." He heads right for the landing outside the bathroom and kneels down to inspect the floor.

Ryan's not buying it. "She'd have to cut a hole in the wood to hide a plastic bag underneath the floor. She'd never do that. Moms are sneaky, but they don't destroy their houses."

I like Ryan's logic. He watches people a lot. I know he's been watching me and Kyler over the whole Celtic-warrior thing. I guess he learns more than he lets on.

"No. She's done something trickier than that," Ryan continues. "She's hidden them somewhere so obvious that you wouldn't even think to look. Like in the closet of your own bedroom, Mikey. No kid ever knows what's in their own closet."

"Genius!" Kyler looks up with a grin. "Pure genius."

Ryan opens my closet. A basketball bounces over his feet, and a box of toy tanks and armored vehicles spills onto the floor. "Was I right or was I right? Your mom could hide an elephant in here." He pulls out the dirty clothes that I stuffed into the closet the last time Mom told me to clean my room, then starts in on a pile of storage boxes.

Kyler's still on his knees on the landing trying to get his pinkie finger down a gap in the floorboards. "I think I got something," he says. "I need wire. Something thin."

"Pencil," I say.

"No, thinner."

"Ruler?"

"Too thick."

"Plastic spear?" Ryan hands him one from a Roman soldier.

"Yeah, that'll work." Kyler gives it a try, but the spear just twangs to a stop in the slot between the boards.

"It's still too thick," he says.

"Door popper," I say.

"What?" Ryan asks.

"Door popper. Mom keeps a special piece of wire on the door ledge over the bathroom. I saw her use it once when Grandpa got stuck. She pulled it down, stuck it in the little hole in the handle, and popped the lock open."

"Worth a try, but hurry," Kyler says.

I drag a chair over to the bathroom. When I reach up, I can just get my fingers to curl around the top of the door ledge. There's something there for sure. I flick my fingertips forward. Something black edges toward me. "Yuck, a spider!" I hate spiders, especially when they're scuttling toward me. I wobble back off the chair and half collapse onto Kyler. One, then two, small dark objects plop to the floor. It takes me a second to recognize what they are. A tiny Brown Bess from my redcoats and, OMG, an awesome assault rifle from my Navy Seals.

"Whoa! You are not going to believe this," I say. Kyler and Ryan are already crowding 'round. "I think I've found them!"

I step back onto the chair and sweep my fingers right along the top of the doorframe. Mini-weapons topple over the edge like a waterfall.

"Let me see!" Kyler picks up a tiny weapon, no bigger than his fingernail, and pretends to fire it. "This is insane, Mikey." He laughs.

Ryan grabs another chair from my room, pulls it into the farthest corner of the landing and stands on tiptoe. "Wow! They're lined up in rows along all the doorframes, Mikey. You've got a whole arsenal here."

"Yes!" I cry. "I knew she wouldn't throw them away."

Ryan drags the chair to Grandpa's room and brushes his fingers across the top of the doorframe, triggering a new cascade of assault rifles and grenade launchers.

"It's raining weapons," Kyler says. On the ledge of every doorframe Mom has lined up the tiny plastic weapons she stole from my soldiers. They scatter to the floor like a military supply drop.

I flex my arms, and I'm about to roar like the Celt when I realize I'd be copying Ryan's dad. That wouldn't be right.

"Sor—" I say, my arms half up in a biceps flex, but I'm interrupted by a woman's voice.

"Ryan, are you there?"

At the bottom of the stairs, Ryan's mom stands in the pool of light spilling out of the kitchen. Her face is white, her eyes are red from crying, but she's smiling, too. Mom and Mariko stand on either side of her, holding her elbows as if she needs steadying on a stormy sea.

From the kitchen I hear Ryan's dad and then Grandpa laughing, "Heh, heh, heh."

Ryan runs down the stairs into a hug. His mom cries. Mariko rubs Ryan's mom's back in small circles. My mom puts her hand on Ryan's shoulder. When Ryan finally pulls away, his mom says, "It's going to be all right. Dr. Curtis says she's found a place for Dad, and it's only an hour away. He's agreed to go, tonight. We'll be able to visit every day…until he's well. Until I'm better, too. We can all go see the doctors there until we work this out."

Mom looks up at us and flashes a quick smile. She's not mad. I guess we did the right thing after all.

"Come talk to your dad," Ryan's mom says.

As they go back into the kitchen, I walk down a few steps and whisper, "Is he really going to be all right?"

Mom closes the kitchen door before she answers. "Mariko seems to think so. She suspects he's suffering not just from post-traumatic stress but other things too…a mixture of things…but they can be treated. He's getting help. That's a big first step." She reaches for the door handle. "Can you two wait upstairs a few more minutes?"

"Sure, Mom." I use my brightest voice, not only because I feel lighter having heard what Mom said, but because this will give Kyler and me time to deal with the mini-guns.

The moment she leaves, I aim for the landing and scoop the guns off the floor.

"What are you doing?" Kyler asks.

"Putting them back. If Mom knows I've found them, she'll hide them somewhere else, and I'll have to find them all over again. This way I can use them whenever I want, and she'll never know. Besides, I don't want to spoil her fun."

Kyler grins. "That is pure genius."

CHAPTER THIRTY-ONE

This afternoon we're presenting our Veterans Day reports, and even Miss O'Brien seems nervous. She's expecting a whole bunch of parents, grandparents, and friends, and she's already called the janitor three times to check that extra chairs will be delivered. But she's nowhere near as nervous as I am. My old report didn't make sense any more. My Celt wasn't a Celt, so I ended up writing my report on Grandpa after all, just like Miss O'Brien had suggested. My stomach twists when I think about reading it aloud. Just like all my reports, it isn't very good. The words never come out right.

Kyler's in charge of putting our artwork on the wall. We've taken the last three weeks of art class to draw charcoal portraits of our veterans. Kyler's portrait of Grandpa is one of the best. Kyler drew him wearing the jungle hat that I found in the shoe box. When Grandpa showed us the hat, I had to pretend I'd never seen it before. In Kyler's portrait, Grandpa seems to be looking right at you. Half of his face is in the shade, and you're not sure whether he's going to burst into tears or laughter. At least, that's what I think.

My portrait is of Grandpa, too. It's not as good as Kyler's, at least I don't think so, but it's much better than my report, that's for sure.

Ryan and I are in charge of the refreshments table. We cover it with a red, white, and blue plastic tablecloth, arrange bowls of crackers and grapes, and set up cups for the lemonade. Ryan keeps glancing at the artwork. He's nervous, too. His dad has been in the treatment program for nearly a month. Ryan wants him to be here today, but doesn't know if he'll come.

Ryan looks at his own picture. He drew a Humvee driving along a dusty road that's scattered with trash. The rest of the class thought it was dumb because it's not a picture of a war veteran, just a car, but I get it. Ryan's veterans are in the Humvee. We can't see them, so we don't even think they're there. But they are. Every day. Driving along roads where one soda can might be the bomb that kills them.

When Ryan finally looks back, I've already lined up the cups. His face is whiter than the paper napkins on the table. I'm wondering what I can say to make him feel better when there's a knock on the door. All the other kids start to talk. Miss O'Brien stands like a soldier at attention. "Ready, class?" she asks.

Casey's mom stares through the small glass panel in the door, talking louder than Casey—if that's possible.

Weird that the moms are so noisy when they're always quieting us down. Casey's mom says something to the other parents waiting with her outside. They burst into laughter as she knocks on the door again.

Miss O'Brien puts her head out and asks for a few more minutes. The parents agree and, at the same time, they wave through the door at their kids. You can feel the excitement. The hairs on my arms bristle. Miss O'Brien keeps her hand on the door as she turns and speaks to us one more time. "Before I let our visitors in, I want you to remember that this is a very special day for you and, more importantly, for some of your guests. Some of the veterans you have written about will be in the audience today, and they may be remembering difficult things and old friends. We need to be respectful." Ryan goes bright red. I think Miss O'Brien notices because she adds, "And I have one more announcement. We have a special guest today. Her name is Dr. Mariko Curtis. Kyler's mom. She works at the veterans' hospital a few blocks away. Some of you know her, I think."

Casey tells everyone she knows Mariko because Mariko comes to a book club at her mom's house. I'm in such a panic I can't say a word. The more Miss O'Brien speaks, the more I realize there's no escape. I don't know if I can do this. My report stinks.

"Dr. Curtis has said that she's interested in displaying

our projects in the main lobby of the hospital. I'm very excited as they will be seen by everyone who visits. This is a great honor, class, but don't get nervous. Just speak clearly and slowly like we practiced."

"Yes, Miss O'Brien," everyone says.

We sit in two lines of chairs and watch the adults file into the room. A few of the moms call out to their kids. The kids smile and wave back. Parents chat to each other while they aim for the front seats. There's a ton of shuffling as people find chairs, pull out phones, or fiddle with the controls on their cameras.

I hear Grandpa arrive even before I see him. "Heh, heh, heh," he laughs. Mariko says, "You're too funny, Marty."

Mom is arm-in-arm with Grandpa. There's something different about her, but I can't think what it is. Maybe it's just that she's smiling. I haven't seen Mom smiling much the last few months. She's always too tired. But today she smiles and gives me a little wave. I stare at her as she takes a seat. Miss O'Brien asks everyone to be quiet. Grandpa sits next to Mom. He winks at me as Miss O'Brien says, "Welcome parents, grandparents, and veterans."

There's no turning back now. My knees go spongy.

Casey's first up, chirping away like a bird. She talks about her mom's co-worker who's in the National Guard.

She trains on the weekend and is super fit. Casey's presentation is really interesting.

Kyler's next. His mom claps before he's even said anything. She's right in the first row holding her neon green smart phone in front of her face. Kyler blushes, drops one of his papers, picks it up again, and clears his throat. He holds his head high so he looks at the people sitting in the back of the room and not at his mom.

He starts by saying that he loves fantasy novels because the characters are always fighting to save their countries or their species. "They're fighting to save their world," he says, "and that's what our veterans do, too." Only Kyler would start a report like that, but he's deadly serious. He goes on to talk about Grandpa fighting in Vietnam, how he lost his leg, how hard it was when he came back because there were war protestors saying the troops shouldn't have been there in the first place. He makes it funny too. He tells Grandpa's favorite story about the exploding can of peaches. When everyone gasps, Grandpa turns around and says, "It's true, every word." The parents laugh out loud and clap. Grandpa takes a bow.

Kyler waits for them to quiet down, just as Miss O'Brien told us to, but in the end he has to talk over the giggles. "But Mr. Andersen says the thing he found hardest about being a soldier was that he missed seeing his daughter grow up. Even when he came back, he wasn't really there for her. He says apart from bringing back his buddies who died, if he could change anything, that's what he'd change."

"And that's true too, Honey Bee," Grandpa whispers, and his eyes fill with tears.

Mom rests her head on his shoulder for a moment and smiles. "Oh, Dad," she says.

The clapping is slow, but it gets louder and louder until everyone has joined in. And they keep on clapping. The parents at the front stand up then the people at the sides and the back, until Mom and Grandpa are surrounded. Everyone nods their head at Grandpa and thanks him for his service.

Kyler turns around and grins. "Cool!"

Mariko smiles and gives Grandpa a pat on the back as everyone shuffles to sit down again. And it's then I see what's different about Mom. She's wearing a new pair of shoes, and they are red. Bright red. Just as red as the little shoes she hid in her closet.

Ryan nudges me in the ribs. "That's you," he whispers. "What?"

"It's your turn."

I've been so busy thinking about Mom and Grandpa that I didn't hear Miss O'Brien talking. "Mr. Andersen is his grandfather," she's saying.

It takes me a while to react.

"Mikey, are you ready?"

I jump to my feet. For a second, I want to push through the chairs and run right out the door. Mom must catch the look on my face because she smiles to reassure me. As she crosses her legs, I catch sight of her bright red shoes again, and I know I have to change my report. I have to say something different from all of the stuff I've written down. My heart thumps as a lava flow of words gushes up my chest.

"My presentation…" I say.

At the back of the classroom, the door cracks open a few inches. Ryan's mom looks in. The door opens further, and she walks in leading Ryan's dad by the hand. His red hair is cut short and spiky. His beard has gone, but he still has a mustache. He looks more like a Celt than ever, but he also looks broad-shouldered, rugged, and every inch a Marine.

Ryan lets out a gasp of surprise as his dad nods at him. Mariko looks up as the door clicks shut and pats the empty chairs next to her. Ryan's mom shakes her head. They stay at the back, leaning against the wall. Miss O'Brien signals that I should start my presentation again.

I look around the room. Pride glitters in Ryan's eyes. Mom whispers in Grandpa's ear. Ryan's dad stands at the back of the room.

"Mikey?" Miss O'Brien prompts.

"Umm, this isn't quite what you're expecting," I put my report down on my chair, "but it's…like…" My face is burning up. "I want to do my presentation about someone in this room…"

Everyone looks at Grandpa expectantly. I catch Ryan staring wide-eyed at his dad, and I look away. I can't risk catching Ryan's eye, or Mom's eye, or anyone's. I look down at the floor and carry on. "Two people actually, who are not called veterans of war, but are veterans all the same. At least, I think they are, because they've gone through a war, but in a different way." I've never felt so stupid. My voice drifts off. I glance at Miss O'Brien. I'm sure her nose is quivering. She must be boiling mad, but I'm wrong. She leans forward and whispers, "Go on, Mikey."

"So, I'm doing my presentation about my mom and my new friend, Ryan O'Driscoll." My voice shakes, but I keep going. "Because when a veteran comes back, the war doesn't stop. A new war starts for them and their families. It's the memories and the sad, bad feelings, and sometimes injuries that we can't even see, that they have to fight this time. My Grandpa says that's because when you're fighting, you don't have time to think and feel or you won't survive. So it's only when you come back home that you realize what happened to you, and what you had to do. It's only then you feel it and relive it. Every day. Even when you're just in the supermarket, or walking down the street."

The room is completely silent, or at least it seems that way to me. *Don't look up, Mikey,* I tell myself. *Just keep going.*

"So, when you are the kid of a veteran, the hard thing is that, sometimes, when your mom or dad comes home they're different for a while. You want to love them just the same way you used to, but you can't. You want your old parent back, but they can't come back—not until they work it all out in their own heads first. It's a hard battle to get back to normal. It's not their fault, and it's not your fault either. It's just hard, and it's even harder when it's a big secret that no one else talks about or understands. So, that's why I think my mom and my friend Ryan are veterans of war, too."

I speak the last line as quickly as I can and sit down. No one claps. No one says anything. Everyone hates me.

Ryan stands straight up. I wonder if he'll get mad at me, right here in front of the whole class, but he just says, "I'm Ryan. My dad is a Marine. He did three tours in Iraq, and I'm really proud of him."

I'm still shaking, and I can't seem to listen to the rest, but I know Ryan is talking about how hard it's been for his dad to come back. When I finally look up,

Ryan's dad has tears in his eyes. No one's glaring at me. They're all listening to Ryan, listening so carefully that even Sawyer's baby sisters are quiet. When I catch my Celt's, I mean Ryan's dad's, eye he mouths, "Thank you." It is the best thing anyone has ever said to me.

I'm jolted out of my thoughts by my name. "Like Mikey said," Ryan finishes up, "it's hard to go to war and it's just as hard getting back home and getting help. I'm doubly proud of my dad because he's done both."

There's a pause.

Then everyone begins to clap. They clap for Ryan and then a little murmur goes around the room. People turn in their chairs to see Ryan's dad standing at the back. Ryan's mom holds his hand tight as his eyes fill. Then he stands tall, nods his head to thank everyone, and puts a finger to each eye to stop the tears. They clap quietly and respectfully at first, but when Ryan's dad smiles, everyone stands and claps and cries.

Ryan sits down and nudges me hard in the ribs. "Wow," he whispers. "Wow."

CHAPTER THIRTY-TWO

That evening we eat at our house, Ryan's family, Kyler's family, my family, and Grandpa's buds. Our projects will be on the walls of the hospital next week and we are all proud. Everyone is talking through the meal, but I can't concentrate. I'm sitting next to Ryan's dad and there's one question I have to ask. I finally blurt it out while Kyler and Ryan are fighting over the last piece of apple pie, and the adults are talking about TV shows.

"Why Cuchulain?" I whisper. "Why did you keep talking about him? I thought you were him." I should bite my tongue out, saying such a stupid thing, but Ryan's dad doesn't seem to mind.

"So did I, when I was a kid. I loved him. My da' told me the stories all the time. I couldn't get enough of them. Those stories saved me in the end," he says, "saved me and confused me too, perhaps. Sounds unbelievable, but when I was in Iraq, I went back to those stories on the bad days, as I patrolled the streets. You see, me and my guys patrolled the road on foot. We had to keep it safe from IEDs, homemade bombs that is. They can go off at any second, anywhere. Sometimes they're hidden in soda cans, or trash. Sometimes they're triggered with a cell phone. They went off every day, were planted anew every day, and I was on the lookout every day. So, I told myself I was like Cuchulain at the ford, fighting a new champion every day. I told myself stories about my life, my fighting, as if I were him. Sounds strange, but you do what you can to survive. You do what makes sense at the time. I even bought myself a torc online, before my third tour, for luck.

"Then, when I came back, I began drinking a lot. It was easier that way." He pauses and looks at Ryan. "Easier for me at least. But then, when the bad memories came, I started to imagine I really was him. I tried to change the stories from mine to his, but they got all mixed up. I'm sorry," he says, leaning out to touch Ryan's arm.

At the end of the meal, Mom asks who wants coffee. All the adults do, especially Grandpa who says that he can't sleep until he's had at least three shots of coffee. "Even better if there's a tot of rum in there, too. Heh, heh, heh." Mom whacks him playfully on the shoulder as she walks to the counter.

While everyone's still talking, Mom beckons me over. She reaches behind the coffee canister and pulls out two things: a copy of *Romanii: Gaulish Explosion*, that's the French version of *Northern Borders* with Vercingetorix as the leader, and a plastic snack bag. "I want you to have these," she whispers, tapping her index finger against her lip in a "shush" sign, so I don't draw attention.

"Oh man! Thanks Mom!" I can hardly control my whisper. It's incredible! *Romanii: Gaulish Explosion* and a bag full of the guns we found above the doorframes. Mom has taken them down herself, and now she's giving them to me.

"Mikey," she says, "I know now that you understand what war's about. I've hidden these all this time, but now I want you to have them."

The bag hovers over my hand. I've dreamed of this moment for years, but now it's here, it's not that big a deal. I know my little soldiers are upstairs waiting to ransack Rome, and I know that Kyler and I will rock *Romanii: Gaulish Explosion*. My money is still on the Celts. I am going to change history. Vercingetorix will never lose again! But right now I say, "Thanks Mom, that's great. But, you know, I think Ryan, Kyler, and I are going to play soccer tonight."

Ryan's dad stands up, one hand on Grandpa's shoulder, one hand on his wife's.

"Maybe I can teach you hurling?" he says. "It's the game of champions."

And we boys shout, "Cuchulain!" all at the same time.

ABOUT THE AUTHOR

When A. E. Conran was Mikey's age she had a tin of tiny Roman and Celtic warriors, which she never finished painting, and a desire to time travel, which remains with her still.

A fan of historical fiction by Rosemary Sutcliff and Henry Treece, she also heard stories from her parents, grandparents, and their friends about living through, and returning from, war.

In addition to writing middle grade novels, A. E. Conran works as a freelance editor, bookseller, book talker, and children's book club facilitator. She lives with her family in Northern California.

Author's Notes

I grew up in a small village in England where there were still veterans of the First World War, one of whom used to walk to the local pub in his medals, greatcoat, and puttees (strips of cloth that First World War soldiers wrapped around their calves). There were also veterans of the Second World War, and even a German Prisoner of War who stayed on in our village after the war ended.

My grandfather, whom I never met, was a career soldier, away for years at a time. My father did his National Service and was an Army Reservist when I was a child. Like many people my age in Britain, I was always aware that people in my family and in families around me had served during wartime.

When I started writing this book, I did not expect one of my main characters, Liam O'Driscoll (the Celt), to be a veteran of a recent war. But as I listened to the news, I became aware of how deeply the wars in Iraq and Afghanistan were affecting a relatively small portion of our society. It struck me how large a gap there was between those who serve and their families, who have given and are still giving so much, and those of us who do not. I sincerely hope this book closes that gap a little.

Liam O'Driscoll (the Celt)

It is important to know that most men and women who return from war will **not** act like Liam. I had to make Liam behave in certain ways so that Mikey and Kyler would continue to believe that he was a Celt. So, I made Liam find it temporarily difficult to tell the difference between what is imaginary and what is real. This can happen, but it is not common.

Some of Liam's symptoms, however, are consistent with the "invisible" effects of war that are recognized by doctors as post-traumatic stress disorder and mild traumatic brain injury. Many people who have served in wars, and their families, are dealing with one or both of these conditions. Doctors are constantly discovering new ways of understanding and treating these invisible injuries. There are excellent resources on the Internet. Please visit my website, www.aeconran.com, for links to more information. I am not a doctor, so I will try to explain these injuries only briefly here. The following information has been taken from www.ptsd.va.gov.

Post-traumatic stress disorder (PTSD), which Grandpa just calls "post-traumatic stress," happens when someone has seen or experienced scary things that they cannot stop thinking about. Sometimes they may have flashbacks, as if they were right back in that scary moment. People with PTSD may have bad dreams and find it hard to sleep; they may be constantly on the look out for danger, even when it is safe; they may avoid situations that remind them of the scary event; and they may startle or react strongly to loud noises or sudden movements, sometimes with anger or frustration. Liam ducks when he hears loud noises. Grandpa still has bad dreams. Both Liam's behavior and Grandpa's dreams could be symptoms of PTSD.

Some doctors might suggest that Liam is also suffering from a **moral injury**, or inner conflict, which is a subset of PTSD. It occurs when someone has had to do, or see, something that may be unavoidable in war, but that goes against that person's beliefs. It can feel like a bruise on your soul that is hard to live with, making it difficult to return to normal life. Liam had to make a very difficult choice, which he would never have had to make at home. Making that choice hurt him and led him to live with a moral injury.

Mild traumatic brain injury (TBI) can be caused by hitting your head or being near an explosion. For a while afterwards this can give you headaches; make you feel tired, depressed, or worried; make you forgetful; or make you very emotional—happy one moment and irritable the next. Liam has been near at least one large explosion. This could explain some of his mood swings.

A Note on Spelling and Pronunciation

The stories of Cuchulain come from Ireland and so the names are spelled and pronounced differently from English names. I have taken the spellings from *The Hound of Ulster*, the book Mikey reads, which uses English versions of the Irish names. One exception is the "Cattle Raid of Cooley," which is called the "Cattle Raid of Quelgney" in *The Hound of Ulster*, and "Táin Bó Cúailnge" in Irish.

Acknowledgements

I started *The Lost Celt* in October 2011, based on a conversation with friends Jeff Kohlwes, Clinical Professor of Internal Medicine and Physician at the University of California, San Francisco, and the Veterans Affairs Medical Center, and Leslie Miya, Adjunct

Professor of Medicine and Attending Physician, Emergency Department, Veterans Affairs Medical Center, San Francisco, California. I am indebted to them for that initial conversation, and to Jeff for reading an early manuscript and trying to help a layperson understand the subtleties of the definitions found in the Author's Notes. Any errors are mine.

During the intervening years many other people have helped with ideas, expertise, encouragement, and financial support. I particularly want to thank one veteran without whom this book would never have been published. You know who you are. How many other "genuses" are out there? Several other veterans also gave financial support anonymously. I thank them and all those who have served, their families, and particularly their children. You have been there for us, and I hope we, the wider community, will be there for you. Twenty percent of the net profits from this book will be donated to veterans' charities.

I fervently hope that the portrayal of Liam O'Driscoll is respectful to veterans dealing with a combination of PTSD and mild TBI, even though, for fictional purposes, it could not be completely typical. Dr. Susan Maxwell, Psychologist, PCT (Post-traumatic Stress Disorders Clinical Team) San Francisco Veterans Affairs Medical Center, read an early draft and helped me greatly with invaluable changes. Nancy Laurenson at the Defense and Veterans Brain Injury Center, Veterans Affairs Palo Alto Health Care System, read a later draft and spent many hours on the telephone helping me understand some of the issues involved.

Josh Gibson, MD, also reassured me that I was on the right track. Thank you all for your time and insight. Any errors in Liam's portrayal are my own.

M'Ladies of the Book (Alie Berka, Darcey Rosenblatt, Lisa Schulman, and Elizabeth Shreeve) read versions of *The Lost Celt*. Ladies, your comments always make my writing better, though we all find it tough at the time. Thank goodness we break for lunch at half past eleven!

Darcey Rosenblatt (so good I named her twice), and Shannon Ledger solved many "but how is this really working" questions. Kathryn Otoshi, Debra Sartell, and Anne Belden, we don't meet as often as we'd like, but it's always wonderful when we do.

The Tuesday Night Writers (Cyndi Cady, Chris Cole, Josh Gibson, Tanya Egan Gibson, Tom Joyce, and John Phillip) and the Pints and Prose regulars have been there for me through the whole journey. So has Jon Wells, who believed in this book like no one else. He talked me through military procedures and let me try on his "cammies." He and our wonderful teacher, Stephanie Moore, are always with the TNWs in spirit.

Joseph and Eleanor Huang, Nathan and Owen Ross, Jackson Walker, and my own Lizzy, read to tell me when clues lay too heavily in the text. Charlie Dyer let me use the name of his playground game "Squash the Tofu," and Ms. Halpern, one of the excellent librarians in the Larkspur-Corte Madera School District, lent me her name for Mikey's librarian.

Katherine Applegate, Eric Elfman, and Suzanne Morgan

Williams graciously put aside valuable time to help and encourage a "pre-published author." Such is the children's book community and the SCBWI. Your kind words and support have made all the difference. Thank you.

I am very fortunate to work for Elaine and Bill Petrocelli at Book Passage in Corte Madera. I am inspired every time I walk through the door, and grateful to Calvin Crosby, Susan Kunhardt, Leslie Berkler, and all the other fabulous staff, for welcoming me so openly and teaching me so much.

And, it was through the Book Passage Children's Writers and Illustrators Conference that I connected with Shirin Yim Bridges, which resulted in me calling myself a "Goose." Thank you, Shirin, for dramatically improving *The Lost Celt* with your editing and for making my dreams come true. Thanks also to my agent, Sarah Davies, my loyal supporter, who allowed me to experiment in the changing world of publishing.

Finally, I'd like to thank my amazing family. Mum and Dad, I was always surrounded by books in your house. Thank you for loving me always. Ben, thanks for initiating me into the ways of boyhood. You are the most charming, imaginative, and wonderful son. Lizzy, you've been my biggest supporter. I would have faltered in my first drafts if it weren't for you, my avid reader and sidekick. I look forward to being your sidekick in the future. Lastly, Pat, all this would have been impossible without you. You are, and always will be, the best thing that ever happened to me.

A. E. Conran, California, June 15, 2015